HIGH PLAINS SHOWDOWN

Young Boone Kingdom killed three renegades who'd murdered his folks, then fled south. Ten years later he returned to West Fork as the lightning-fast Hondo Kid, and was caught up in a range war. Tough cattleman Roberto Aguandra intended to wrest High Plains from horse-rancher Isaac Haynes. But why had Aguandra waited ten years to make his move? Hot lead would fly before Boone could solve an old mystery and finally bring peace to a troubled range.

WILL KEEN

HIGH PLAINS SHOWDOWN

Complete and Unabridged

LINFORD
Leicester

First published in Great Britain in 1999 by
Robert Hale Limited
London

First Linford Edition
published 2000
by arrangement with
Robert Hale Limited
London

British Library CIP Data

Keen, Will
  High plains showdown.—Large print ed.—
Linford western library
1. Western stories
2. Large type books
I. Title
823.9'14 [F]

ISBN 0–7089–5689–0

Published by
F. A. Thorpe (Publishing)
Anstey, Leicestershire

Set by Words & Graphics Ltd.
Anstey, Leicestershire
Printed and bound in Great Britain by
T. J. International Ltd., Padstow, Cornwall

This book is printed on acid-free paper

Prologue

Young Boone Kingdom heard the rattle of gunfire when he was more than a mile from the cabin, riding his tough little paint up in the naked hills above the thick timber. The sounds could have been the crackle of a fire, or the distant snapping of dry twigs.

At first he thought his pa had ridden up after him, even looked across expecting to see him emerge from the edge of the dark woods sitting tall and straight atop his big blue roan.

Then realization hit him like a hammer blow: someone was attacking their homestead, and Pa was in trouble. It was as if all the breath had been driven from his body. Suddenly his throat was tight, his heart hammering in his chest. His clear grey eyes already wide in anticipation of the horrors he was to witness, he lashed the pony into a fast gallop and headed back down the rocky slope.

He sent the paint into the trees at breakneck pace and without any thought for his own danger, the wind flattening his old hat brim and ballooning his shirt, the game little horse's hooves drumming along the familiar trails that snaked down through the timber, and all the while his mind strained ahead to the log cabin on the edge of the meadow and his throat ached at the memory of the way it was when he left.

He held on to those memories, Boone Kingdom, for, from early childhood, he had trembled at the cold-blooded brutality of the renegades who roamed that part of west Texas and knew with a feeling of physical sickness that when he reached the cabin, memories were all he would have left in the world.

Ma had been heading for the creek, he recalled, her long dark hair falling about her shoulders as she brushed through the dew-soaked grass to fetch water to wash their worn work-clothes. Pa had been swinging the long handled axe out back by the open fronted outhouse, the gleaming blade clunking into the soft timber, his shirt sleeves rolled back from brawny arms as he chopped logs to replenish the pile before moving out into the fields.

Boone Kingdom had looked back and waved as he rode away, and at that thought his clamped lips twitched in a half smile that masked pain that was like a knife twisting in his heart.

Then those memories and the smile were torn cruelly from him as the dappled sunlight heralding the edge of the woods fell across his face and, like something out of a nightmare, the harsh tang of wood-smoke came to torment his flared nostrils and paralyse his mind with a new terror.

Out of that terrible fear, like good out of evil, came common sense. Every nerve in his body screamed at him to bolt headlong out of the woods and fling himself upon whatever horrors had come riding out of the western wilderness to tear his family apart. But the wisdom drilled into him by his father over countless lamplit supper-tables told him to rein in, to stay hidden in the woods.

'*Son,*' big John Kingdom had drummed into him time and time again, '*there ain't nothing in this world more sad and of less use to folk than a dead hero.*'

Young Boone Kingdom waited.

Though the cabin was close, all but the top of the stone chimney was hidden by a low grassy rise that swelled up from the willows alongside the swift-flowing Coldwater Creek. Within the comforting stillness of the trees, harsh voices drifted to him. Strange voices. Voices that caused a cold shiver to ripple down his spine as he backed the paint deeper into the woods. And over those voices there now came a fierce crackling, the deep, devouring roar of flames, and gradually the dappled

4

sunlight that filtered through the trees faded to a false dusk as smoke billowed high across the meadow.

★ ★ ★

The pall of smoke had thinned to a slender white column that rose straight into the clear blue skies when they rode out, their savage work done. Boone Kingdom caught sight of them from a distance, three ragged strangers wearing floppy hats, two dark, one dove-grey, their faces unshaven and all about them the glitter of weapons.

He left the woods, then, and as the paint carried him over the grassy rise, he closed his eyes in a moment of the purest agony and the blood drained from his face as his mind snapped shut like a steel trap.

And because he knew from warm, whispered conversations overheard when the snug oil lamps of night-time had been extinguished, that they wanted their last resting place to be on the rise overlooking Coldwater Creek and the soft grey willows, it took Boone Kingdom most of that fiercely hot day to bury his ma and pa.

* * *

One old man who had witnessed the killing, hunkered down in the crackling dead leaves, eagle-sharp eyes watchful as he chewed a plug of tobacco and stroked his stained and tangled beard, stayed inside the woods just long enough to make sure the boy was safe. Then he spat a final stream of sour juice into the soggy brown mess between his ragged moccasins, climbed aboard his mule, and rattled off on a trail that would eventually take him through Colorado and Wyoming to Stillwater, in the Beartooth Mountains of Montana.

* * *

For some reason the killers came back when the red ball of the sun had sunk behind the purple smudge of the Sierra Grande, and the dampening meadows and woods and the smouldering remains of the Kingdoms' homestead were bathed in that strange luminous half light that casts no shadows.

The three men came riding carelessly down the wide trail that dropped steeply past the rocky west bluff and skirted the grove of tall pines that stretched almost as far as the cabin, bridles jingling, horses blowing, their coarse laughter carried unnaturally loud on the cool evening breeze.

This time Boone Kingdom was ready. His pa's gunbelt had been carefully rolled up on the stack of old oil cans and shiny hand-tools in the shed. Boone buckled it about his slim waist, used the supple rawhide thongs to tie the two holsters to his thighs and, at the natural hang of the two guns, he knew that while he had not yet attained his pa's bulk, he had already surpassed his height.

He was standing tall and straight in

the centre of the trail, a slender boy bearing a grown man's deadly weapons, when the three riders jogged up out of the rutted dip past the last of the pines and fixed him with their dark eyes. His hands were relaxed at his sides, his fingertips brushing the warm oiled leather of the holsters, his palms close to the smooth wooden butts of the twin Remington .44s.

In stature he was a boy, but shining bright in his mind was the belief that he was already a great gunman, for another thing his pa had taught him was that most things in life are settled by the thoughts a man holds in his head. So, planted firmly in Boone Kingdom's mind — thrust deeper and firmer into his consciousness with each agonizing bite of the spade as he dug two graves on that lonely ridge — there was the conviction that he was not just a great gunman, but the fastest gunman that ever lived.

Yet still he watched the approach of the renegades who had murdered his ma and pa with something close to terror eating away at his innards. He had expected that feeling, and accepted it. *A man who refuses to admit to fear*, his pa had told him, *is not a man but a fool*, and these men were dangerous killers.

'Hell,' one of them growled. 'It's just a kid.' And Boone Kingdom allowed himself a small, inward smile, because the long day's digging told him this man was wrong.

'An orphan now, I guess,' another said, and sniggered.

They rode close, formed a half circle and reined in, their blank eyes taking in the tied down sixguns.

From New Mexico, Boone Kingdom surmised from their appearance. Rode across the border, then along Carrizo Creek, drunk on tequila, looking for some fun, came across a good man who would have shown no fear.

'How old are you, boy?'

The question was asked hoarsely by a big man with a wide sombrero shading the scarred face of a bandit.

'Fifteen,' Boone Kingdom said.

'Didn't your pappy tell you to call a man sir when you're spoke to?'

'When I see a man,' Boone Kingdom said, holding tight onto his voice, 'I'll be happy to do that.'

'Well now.' The big man eased his weight in the saddle, turned his head to spit. He looked at the lean rider on his left who had eased a shotgun out of his saddle scabbard and now rested it across his pommel; turned to the much younger man on his right who wore a dove-grey hat that was a shade too big for him and who had backed his horse around so that he had a clear and unimpeded view of the boy.

To Boone Kingdom, wise beyond his years, it seemed that in the uncertain gaze of that younger man as he cast his eyes over the smouldering ruins he detected indecision, and fear. And because that wisdom told him that no man should be frightened when

10

confronted by one so young, he began wondering.

Then the big renegade laughed. 'So if we ain't men — in your humble opinion — why don't you tell us what you see in front of you?'

'I see three killers,' Boone Kingdom said. 'And one of 'em's wearing my pa's hat.'

'Then if we're killers,' the big man said, anger flaring, 'let's get on with the killin',' — and he went for his gun.

For Boone Kingdom, it was as if from that moment time stood still. For the three killers, the fraction of a second they had left moved with a speed that was unexpected, and fatally bewildering.

Kingdom saw the big man's hand dip fast and with practised ease to his holster and start back up with a big blued Dragoon. He saw the blur of movement as the young man wearing John Kingdom's hat went through the beginnings of a clean, fast draw — and

11

with chilling calm he ignored both men.

The terror had faded into the background. His body remained balanced, utterly still. There was no perceptible movement of his forearms, but in the one moment his hands were empty, in the next they were holding the twin Remingtons and both muzzles were spitting flame.

So unbelievably fast was Boone Kingdom's double draw that bullets from both six-guns slammed into the man with the shotgun before his finger could so much as twitch on the triggers. His lean body was still absorbing the double shock — still starting on a movement that would take him backwards out of the saddle — when the twin Remingtons shifted a few degrees and again their muzzles flared.

By comparison with what young Boone Kingdom had already achieved in front of the smoking ruins of his home the two remaining gunmen were like men dragging their right arms clear of thick, clinging mud. They had made their draw before Boone Kingdom moved, but still they were a lifetime too slow.

Their six-guns were clearing their holsters when the twin Remingtons sang their song of death. They were lifting but still pointing uselessly towards the packed earth when the big man took a heavy slug in the throat and choked on his own blood and, under the hat stolen from the dead homesteader, a black hole appeared in the centre of the boy's forehead.

The three renegades were dead when they hit the ground. Their bodies thumped heavily and as one into the dust, for there had been no perceptible interval between Boone Kingdom's four shots.

As the thunder of gunfire faded, a heavy, eerie silence settled over the ruined Kingdom homestead and the low, grassy hillock.

That silence was broken by the

crunch of Boone Kingdom's boots in the dust. He turned his back on the smouldering ruins of his home, walked stiffly over to the man with a bullet hole between his eyes and crouched down beside him. And as his eyes brimmed with hot tears that spilled to fall like rain into the staring eyes of the dead young man, Boone took his pa's hat in both hands, lifted it high, and planted it firmly on his own head.

★ ★ ★

The man whose horse had thrown a shoe three miles back down the trail watched in disbelief from the edge of the rocky bluff. He was gazing east, from a distance. The four figures in front of the smouldering ashes were indistinct, bathed in the soft light of evening.

To the watcher, from his distant vantage point, it was as if nothing moved. He saw three men ride up out of the hollow and rein in. Then,

14

after several moments of stillness, as if in slow motion, they toppled from their saddles.

As they fell, the rattle of gunfire reached the watcher's ears, and he realized what had happened — but still did not believe.

It was 1858.

Four men had witnessed the birth of a legend but, fittingly, only one lived to tell the tale.

1

West Fork was a town that sprang up in the high undulating grassland between the waters of Coldwater and Rita Blanca Creeks in the Texas Panhandle and spent the next twenty years wondering what the hell it was doing there. For part of that time it had contracted as many of the old folks who'd drifted down from the Santa Fe Trail and built the town around an abandoned soddy had become discontented, packed up and moved on.

To Boone Kingdom's critical eye as he looked down on it in the late evening sunshine it had grown considerably in the years since he'd rattled down the settlement's main street on the first pony he'd ever owned. That suggested prosperity from some source, which in the Panhandle surely meant cattle. The big drives had started a year ago, but mostly from southern Texas by way of the Chisholm Trail. Whoever had moved into the grassland around West Fork had the advantage of being closer to the booming Kansas cow towns, and appeared to have brought new soul to a town that had lost all hope.

From his high vantage point he could see the flapping skins of abandoned tarpaper shacks on the outskirts, a few clothes lines hung with white linen indicating inhabited dwellings closer in. The wide, dusty street was a shadowy canyon flanked by the false-fronted buildings from where the regenerated town's enterprising businessmen fed and watered men and horses, looked after their money, locked them up when they got drunk and planted them six feet under when — for one reason or another — they quit breathing.

Nothing had changed, yet everything had changed. He was a man returning to his home town a stranger. After ten years how many familiar faces remained, he wondered, among the new? How many of the older residents remained; how many of those remembered, or cared?

It took him ten minutes to make the easy ride down from the ridge, and in that short time the sun dragged its blazing upper rim down behind the purple mountains of New Mexico and he rode in off the plains bathed in light that was like liquid gold reflected from the soaring canopy of high clouds.

He made his entrance into the shaded main street of West Fork the way he rode into every town, walking the powerful sorrel gelding down the centre of the street, slack reins held in gloved hands that rested lightly on the horn, his grey eyes observant without ever openly staring.

Oil lamps were already casting their yellow glow from windows up and down the street. A piano tinkled, off key, and two 'punchers rode up to the half dozen or so horses at the hitch rail outside the Breaker saloon, talking loudly as they tied up. A door slammed under an overhang and a man in a dark suit stepped down from the plankwalk outside a building Kingdom figured was still home to the town's only lawyer. This was the same man, more than likely, only now his thick dark hair would be flecked with grey. The lawyer — if it was he — headed across the street at an angle, and Boone Kingdom let his eyes flick ahead and saw the open door of the stone building that was the marshal's office and jail, lamplight shining on a glossy pair of boots hitched onto a desk top.

Then Kingdom was off the street and in the cool, sweet-scented runway of the livery, and a gnarled man he remembered with affection was limping out of the office and looking at him with familiar, crinkled grey eyes that held not recognition, but suspicion and wariness.

'Look after him,' Kingdom said gruffly as he slid down, and had to bite his tongue to hold back the name.

'The best oats, a good rub down, a clean stall for the night.'

'Every one of 'em's clean,' the old man growled, and Boone Kingdom smelt the drink on his breath, saw the redness in the weak blue eyes. The grizzled head was cocked, birdlike, as the hostler squinted up at Kingdom. 'I ain't bein' pushy, mind — but don't I know you from somewhere?'

For an instant Kingdom was caught off guard. Then he saw the swift glance down at the twin Remingtons in their tied-down holsters, remembered the suspicion in the wise old eyes and suspected that if Dusty Rhodes recognized him at all, it was as a breed, not an individual.

'If you do,' he said quietly, 'it's knowledge you should keep under your hat, old timer.'

He saw the grimace that was almost a snarl of contempt, took a gold coin from his pocket and tossed it to the old hostler then turned, and set off across the street.

It was a long trail he had ridden. He was tired and not quite sure what he intended to do in West Fork; not yet convinced that he would stay. But the words he had spoken to the hostler were the first he had uttered to a human in more than a week and issued from a parched throat, and the dry taste of trail dust in his mouth now directed his footsteps.

He skirted the dozing horses, climbed the creaking steps and pushed through the swing doors of the Breaker saloon.

The murmur of conversation faltered, then picked up. Kingdom stepped inside and surveyed the interior of the one building in West Fork his pappy had never let him enter.

Cigarette smoke was a heavy pall threatening to dim the hanging oil lamps. Three or four 'punchers were bellied up to the long bar, watched with lazy insolence by the scantily clad woman in the enormous oil painting hung over the back shelves. Elsewhere in the room there were several round tables, a larger one occupied by four men who smoked fat cigars and who had all glanced around at Kingdom's entrance. A wide door at the far end led through to an unlighted second area — dining-room, faro tables? — and on a small platform in the back corner a man was bent over the piano Kingdom had heard as he rode into town.

A dozen pairs of eyes furtively watched his progress as he made his way to the bar, loose-bored Mexican spur rowels jingling, but it was a reaction Kingdom had become used to as his reputation grew. Like the hostler, the occupants of the saloon recognized his type, not his face. But because some of the men here were younger, and perhaps carried their six-guns with challenging arrogance, they would understand that this man was no ordinary gunman.

'Beer,' Kingdom told the tall barman, and a glass of foaming liquid was quickly placed before him and as quickly gulped down. The barman's eyes flickered with amusement. A bony hand tipped the big jug and a second glass replaced the first. Kingdom nodded his thanks, scooped it up and turned to face the room.

He was a tall, lithe man, Boone Kingdom, with wide shoulders tapering down to a slender waist. Hair the colour of sun-bleached corn poked thickly and untidily from beneath a worn dove-grey Stetson that shaded clear, remarkably penetrating eyes of a grey that could twinkle with laughter or take on the hardness of cold steel. The face was lean and weather-worn, high of cheekbone, with a strong jaw and a mouth that was set firm now but also suggested that here was a man always likely to break into rich laughter.

From the faded blue bandanna around the strong throat, the dusty vest, the cotton shirt, the cord pants hanging loose over tan leather boots — everything about Boone Kingdom was worn with age.

But the butts of the twin Remingtons

hanging low on each thigh in tied-down, oiled leather holsters, were worn smooth from frequent handling, and it was the sight of these that now warned those men covertly glancing in his direction that a quick once-over was all this stranger would tolerate.

A match flared as a 'puncher at the bar fired a cigarette. Then the piano swung into a lively polka as the swing doors slapped open and the man in the dark suit Kingdom had seen cross the street came in. He made his way through the tables, was met at the other end of the room by a striking, dark-haired woman in a red dress who emerged from the shadows beyond the wide door, stood on tiptoe to kiss him, then flashed a brilliant smile at the grinning pianist.

Dave van Tinteren. Lawyer. Aged some, but still upright and dapper. Had seemingly spent several minutes chinwagging with the marshal in his office, and Kingdom caught himself wondering if it was just passing the time of day.

Conscious of the barman behind him, Kingdom said without turning, 'That group at the table. What are they, town council, cattlemen's association?'

'Rocking Z, big cattle ranch up close to the New Mex border. Two of 'em, anyhow. Big feller with curly black hair's Roberto Aguandra, moved in from New Mexico, owns the spread. Man opposite him with the face chipped out of hard rock's his foreman, Harry Gregg.'

'The others?'

'Karl Tanner owns the bank. I guess all that figurin' put on weight and made his hair fall out. Other feller's Aguandra's son, like two peas in a pod only the youngster ain't got his pa's brains. Married a local gal, took over a small disused spread out on Coldwater Creek.'

'The old Kingdom homestead?'

'The same.'

'Well, how about that,' Kingdom

said softly. He studied the back of the younger Aguandra's head for a moment or two, let his eyes drift and said, 'What about that salty character over by the window, black hair turnin' grey, wearin' buckskins, looks like he's made of whang leather left too long in the sun?'

'Isaac Haynes. Runs horses. His spread's also on Coldwater, ranch called High Plains, some miles west of the old Kingdom place.'

'So Roberto Aguandra runs the Rocking Z, his son moves into the Kingdom place and Haynes's runnin' mustangs smack dab in the middle.'

'Yeah,' the barman said. 'Interestin', ain't it? And don't look now, Kid, but someone over at that table is requesting your presence.'

The big man, Roberto Aguandra, had turned towards the bar and lifted a heavy hand glittering with gold rings to summon Kingdom.

'You called me Kid,' Kingdom said, deliberately turning his back on

27

Aguandra to fix the barman with his level grey eyes.

The barman grinned easily. 'You were seen over at Dusty Rhodes's stable. Your name beat you through the door by a good five minutes. The Hondo Kid — right? Fastest gun since . . . hell, since forever!'

Kingdom pursed his lips. 'Don't seem to bother you none. But I guess all kinds walk in here wanting nothing more than something wet to throw down their throats.' Kingdom's gaze took in the amusement that seemed a permanent fixture in the dancing blue eyes and he said, 'Most bartenders I've met keep their ears open, their mouths shut. If I need you, who do I ask for?'

'Gus'll serve the purpose,' the barman said, extending his hand. 'Maybe both of us've got secrets.'

Kingdom shook the outstretched hand, said, 'Where's this feller brought the good news of my coming?'

'Ed Jaffe?' Gus shrugged. 'Made his

announcement, went right back out. Could be he's got some big ideas about makin' a name for himself before you leave town.'

Then his eyes flicked past Kingdom's shoulder as a voice struggling through a throat scarred by too many cigars and too much strong liquor growled, 'It ain't often I walk across the floor to talk to a man who's deliberately insolent.' Kingdom swung around to find himself face to face with an exasperated Roberto Aguandra.

'So why do it now?'

'Because the word got around that the Hondo Kid's something special.'

'The word is right — but walking all the way over here to tell me something everybody knows is wasting your time, and mine.'

Now the conversation in the saloon did stutter to a halt. The pianist fingered a strident discord, staggered into a slow waltz and bent lower over the keys as if to make a smaller target. Someone coughed nervously. A chair scraped, and the hot air seemed to quiver with tension.

And over by the window, Isaac Haynes snorted loudly and derisively, rose up and heeled his chair out of the way, then stomped out of the saloon.

Roberto Aguandra's frown deepened as his eyes examined Kingdom. His black hair was damp with sweat, his handsome, fleshy face red beneath the tan. He was an inch shorter than Kingdom's six two, but built like an average sized ox. The clothing he wore was ordinary range garb, but expensive, and not spoiled by too much hard work.

'Listen, Hondo,' he said bluntly, the faint Mexican accent thickened by smouldering anger, 'I don't think too much of men who hide behind a fancy name they plucked out of a hat.'

'If I had another name it died with my ma and pa,' Kingdom said, 'so you're still wasting time, Aguandra.'

Aguandra grunted. 'All right,' he said impatiently, 'so why don't you put that cheap beer back on the bar, come over and sample some of Gus's best whiskey while we talk?'

'Is that a style of living I should get used to?' Kingdom suggested.

'You play your cards right — sure, why not.'

Arrogantly taking the invitation as accepted, Aguandra turned away and strode back to his companions. Kingdom looked at Gus, shrugged, took the empty jolt glass he was handed and walked with it to Aguandra's table.

Aguandra was already seated. He gestured to a chair, waited until Kingdom had swung one around and straddled it then waved an arm and said, 'Karl Tanner. Harry Gregg, my foreman. My son, Ric. You already know my name.'

'For what it's worth,' Kingdom said, and as Aguandra let the insult slide by with nothing more than a cold glance he leaned across the back of his chair and filled his glass from the bottle.

'What the hell do we want with a

cheap gunslinger?' Ric Aguandra said, and Kingdom looked across at the younger man and mockingly raised his glass.

'Seems like your pa forgot to wash your mouth out with lye soap this morning, boy,' he said, and saw the thick body tense, the dark eyes narrow with disbelief, noted the sudden, swift movement from Harry Gregg as he slammed his left forearm across the younger Aguandra's chest.

'This ain't gettin' us anywhere,' Gregg said.

Under a felt hat that carried the dust of a thousand long trails the foreman's square face had been made rugged by wind and weather and a score of harsh encounters with man and beast. His dragoon moustache was sweeping and ragged, the pale eyes watchful but not interested. The big left hand was missing a finger; the strength in the arm that held back Ric Aguandra was an indication of this rugged Westerner's quiet power.

'So why don't *you* tell me where it's supposed to be taking us,' Kingdom said quietly, 'and leave them to get on with their braggin'?'

'When you get up to walk out of here, reflect on the fact that a reputation don't make you immortal,' Harry Gregg said.

'But for some reason it makes powerful men fall over themselves to buy me drinks,' Kingdom said, 'and until a couple of minutes ago there were two people in this room'd like to know why.'

'What two?' Roberto Aguandra snapped.

'Me, and the feller called Isaac Haynes who just walked out in disgust,' Kingdom said blandly, and heard Ric Aguandra's muttered curse, saw the sudden flare of interest in the lean foreman's eyes.

'What the hell do you know about Haynes?' Roberto Aguandra gritted. He was leaning forward now, his hands flat on the table, his eyes ugly.

'About as much as I know about you, which considerin' I've been in town less than an hour, ain't a lot,' Kingdom said. He drained his glass, dismounted from the chair he was straddling and stepped away from the table. 'What I do know is based on the same information you're using to judge me: hearsay and appearance. Maybe we've both got it right, in which case, God help us. The next few days should tell — but whichever way it turns out, it should be interesting.'

He nodded to Harry Gregg, pointedly ignored both the glowering Aguandras and walked out of the saloon into the cool night.

2

Boone Kingdom stood on the plankwalk outside the Breaker saloon and gratefully inhaled deep lungfuls of the cooling air while prudently standing well back in the shadows and letting his gaze sweep up and down the street.

Oil lamps creaked on rusted brackets as they swung lazily in the light breeze. From this side of the street he could see Dusty Rhodes's livery stable almost directly opposite; the West Fork Bank was some forty yards away adjoining what he remembered was Dave van Tinteren's office, the town's only hotel was close by. Some shouting and laughter was drifting faintly from the town's second saloon, Slocombe's, situated on the town's western outskirts.

Kingdom pulled out the makings, leisurely built himself a smoke; heard the saloon's swing doors slap back and forth as someone stepped outside.

Unexpectedly, almost at his shoulder, a match flared.

'It's been a long time, Boone.'

Kingdom reached up to take hold of the man's wrist, brought the hand holding the match closer to his face and touched the flame to his cigarette. Then he blew smoke and, as the match was flicked away, he looked at the tall man in the dark suit and said, 'Too long, Dave, but in all that time some things ain't changed.'

The lawyer chuckled. 'I can name a few. Sorting out other people's legal problems put grey into my hair as well as money in the bank. Rheumatism got to Dusty Rhodes, made him even more cantankerous and much too fond of the bottle. You rode out of here a kid with a broken heart, came back a grown man.'

'But still you recognized me.'

'No; I recognized the guns, Boone. And if that sounds crazy, those

Remington New Model Army .44s were patented in '58, and over in my office there's a polished wooden box lined with red felt that's been lying empty since the day I gave the two you're packing to your pa.'

Kingdom sighed. 'I never knew that,' he said softly.

'Only one other man ever did. If you imagine Dusty didn't recognize those guns, you'd better think again.'

'That saddens me,' Kingdom said, and meant it. 'I read contempt in his eyes, thought it was for just another two-bit gunman passing through. I guess he was letting me know he was disgusted I'd chosen that particular road to travel.'

'Talking of travelling — why *did* you come back to West Fork?'

'I had a dream,' Boone Kingdom said. He lightly touched Dave van Tinteren's arm and together they moved off along the plankwalk at a slow walk, the cigarette glowing in Kingdom's gloved right hand.

'I never thought too much about it, but in a man's memory, time stands still. It was in my thoughts to ride out to the old spread and find things exactly as they were. Same blackened timber where the cabin stood. Same two graves up on the hill above the willows, maybe overgrown some now but otherwise unchanged.'

'Then you got talking to Roberto Aguandra,' van Tinteren said, understanding in his voice.

'Not Aguandra — Gus. He told me Ric Aguandra moved onto the old place, had himself a new wife.'

Dave van Tinteren's eyes were searching. 'Ten years is a long time, Boone. Aguandra's wife is a girl sat next to you at school, always said — '

'Hondo!'

The shout came from close behind them, harsh, challenging, but pitched that shade too high and with a crack in it that told of tight strung nerves.

'Get out of the way, Dave,' Kingdom said. 'I was expectin' this.'

He pushed the startled lawyer towards the street, flicked his cigarette into the dust then turned slowly to look back the way they had come.

Ten yards away, a man had stepped out of a doorway. The bright lights from the Breaker saloon turned him into a black silhouette, legs spread, right arm hooked, hand curled close to the six-gun jutting from his right hip.

'Ed Jaffe?'

'That's my name. After tonight everyone'll know it. This is the end of the road for the Hondo Kid.'

'You've been readin' too many of Buntline's dime novels, son.'

'Ain't read a book in my whole life, so quit talkin', Kid, and make your play.'

'This is getting more damn foolish by the minute.'

'Hell, you're scared, ain't you! The great Hondo Kid's got a yeller streak down his back!' There was a note of hysteria in Jaffe's voice as he blustered, then broke into a cackling laugh. His head swung wildly from side to side, seeking witnesses to his fearless confrontation. But Dave van Tinteren had faded away into the night and, as if the quiet was that presaging a violent storm, the street was empty.

'Not yellow,' Boone Kingdom said quietly. 'It's just I never did like shootin' an unarmed man.'

Jaffe snorted. 'What the hell are you talkin' about? I've got a six-gun on my hip, so pull your iron and — '

'You're mistaken,' Kingdom cut in flatly.

From the direction of the marshal's office a strident voice bellowed, 'You two, cut that out!'

It came too late.

Ed Jaffe was still poised in a half crouch with his body tensed for the fast draw that would make him famous when Kingdom's six-guns seemed to leap into his hands. He triggered twice, the twin blasts deafening, the muzzle flashes blinding in the evening gloom. Both bullets tore into Jaffe's holster where it met his belt, ripping through the tough leather and sending the startled Jaffe staggering off balance.

In the moment of stunned silence as the fading echoes of the gunshots slapped off the town's false fronts, Kingdom saw the would-be gunman's eyes widen in shock. Then, feeling no pain, realizing no hot lead had slammed into his flesh and believing, mistakenly, that the Hondo Kid had fired and missed, Ed Jaffe slapped leather.

But the holster had gone. With amusement Kingdom watched Jaffe's palm slap his thigh, then comically paw his leg in a frantic search for a six-gun that was hanging upside down below his knee, held there by the holster's tie-down thong.

'Judas Priest!'

Something hard jabbed into Boone Kingdom's backbone as the voice growled in amazement close to his ear. Then Ed Jaffe's pistol slid from the inverted holster and clunked to the boards.

'Go home, Ed, while you're still in one piece,' the voice growled.

Without a word Jaffe stooped, picked up his pistol, walked stiffly along the plankwalk to the hitch rail and flung himself atop a ragged dun. Seconds later, the pony's hooves were rattling down the street, leaving a veil of drifting dust.

'If a man keeps his eyes open there's something new to see every day.'

The hard pressure left Kingdom's back and he turned to face a short, stocky man with a crooked smile on his craggy face that left his blue eyes hard and watchful. A gleaming badge was pinned to his vest. His big hand eased down the Colt's hammer, and he lifted the pistol apologetically.

'A precautionary measure in case you planned on practisin' the same fancy shootin' on his ears.'

'I was tempted,' Kingdom said, 'but a slight misjudgement would have left him dead, not lame.'

'You'll get a second chance,' the marshal said, holstering the .45. 'Let's you and me go have a talk.'

Several men pushed through the saloon's swing doors as they set off down the street, warm light flooding the plankwalk and carrying with it the hum of conversation and the lively tinkling of the piano. Almost at once two horses drummed past, and Kingdom recognized the bulky figure of Roberto Aguandra, the rangy outlines of his foreman, saw them stare across and noted the glitter of Aguandra's eyes, the almost imperceptible nod of Crabtree's head.

Another horse made off in the opposite direction. The younger Aguandra, heading for home, Kingdom guessed, and at the thought he tasted bitterness, then deliberately blanked his mind.

The door of the marshal's office was wide open, the blue veil of smoke from the cigar he had hurriedly extinguished still curling around the brass oil lamp.

He followed Kingdom inside, kicked the door shut, gestured to a chair then took his place in an old leather swivel chair behind a heavy desk that stood alongside an iron safe and half-a-dozen racked Winchesters and shotguns.

His tooled leather boots slammed back into a groove years of similar moves had worn into the oak surface of his desk. One hand reached out to a fancy ceramic humidor and extracted a thin cigar that looked as dry as a cowchip. The other plucked a match from a vest pocket, a thumbnail snapped it alight, and within seconds the harsh aroma of strong tobacco filled the room.

That done, he poked a finger at a small carved plaque on the desk that read MARSHAL JIM CRABTREE, pushed it so it faced his visitor and squinted at Kingdom.

'All right,' he said, and coughed harshly. 'So why didn't you kill him, do your reputation some good?'

'Killing a fool like Jaffe would have

been murder, and you know it. Some good that would have done. And what the hell's a reputation, anyway?'

'Go on,' Crabtree said. 'You tell me.'

'Hearsay, Marshal. Words distorted by being told too many times around too many different camp-fires, by men who were someplace else when it mattered. I already said pretty much the same to Roberto Aguandra.'

Jim Crabtree sucked wetly at the cigar, gestured with the glowing, smouldering tip and said, 'Forget Aguandra for a minute, Hondo. What I'm sayin' is, like with this stogie, there ain't no smoke without fire. What I know for sure is you were maybe sixteen, seventeen when you showed up in Sonora, or maybe it was Chihuahua. Who cares? Fact is you hung around long enough to prove you was greased lightnin' with a six-gun — in either or both hands — then crossed the Bravo and over the next some years built yourself a reputation that stretched from Laredo clear up to the Nations.'

'Two reputations,' Kingdom said.

Crabtree trickled smoke, nodded slow agreement. 'Yeah. Half the population of Texas had the Hondo Kid down for a cold-blooded killer. The other half swore he never pulled an iron 'less the other man's gun was up and cocked.' Eyes speculative, he said softly, 'But either way if a man came up against you he was as good as dead — which finally brings us around to Roberto Aguandra.'

Boone Kingdom stretched out his long legs, crossed his ankles, dug out his tobacco sack and began to fashion a cigarette. The old swivel chair creaked as Crabtree leaned wide to reach sideways. He took a bottle off the top of the safe, grunted as he bent to slide open a desk drawer, came up with two smeared glasses. He pulled the cork with his teeth, slopped raw whiskey into the glasses, slid one towards Kingdom.

'Did Aguandra try to hire you — or

was he just testing the water?'

Kingdom's brow creased in an exaggerated frown. 'I don't understand.'

'I guess he was testing the water — but sure you know what I'm talking' about, it ain't all that damn hard to figure out.' Crabtree toyed with his glass, flicked ash from the cigar into a cow's hoof ashtray. 'Rancher moved in maybe eight, nine years ago, took himself a slice of land along the border, breathed life into West Fork. His boy done the same, only more recent and some ways to the east. Now Roberto'd like to expand in that direction, make one helluva big spread. He might succeed — most likely would — but for a time things'd get a mite rough. Be too small a fight to call a range war, but plenty big enough to see a heap of blood spilled.' He shook his head, looked up sharply from under his thick eyebrows. 'What I'm sayin' is, all of that could be avoided . . . .'

As Crabtree's voice trailed off — clearly an invitation for the other

47

man to fill in what he'd left unfinished — Kingdom looked at his cigarette, stuck it between his lips, then changed his mind, unhooked his legs and leaned forward to spend time mashing the quirly in the ashtray alongside the marshal's boots.

He couldn't figure Jim Crabtree. First thing a marshal should have done was run a rogue gunman out of town. What Crabtree did was apologize for being too aggressive with his six-gun, invite him into his office, set him in a chair with a drink then begin a rambling monologue about a local rancher's ambitions and problems.

Was he in Roberto Aguandra's vest pocket? Had the hurried nod of the head as Aguandra and Gregg rode by been a signal that he'd follow up whatever Aguandra had started? And if that was the case, what the hell had Isaac Haynes got going for him that was forcing a powerful rancher to hire a professional gunman instead of simply moving in and taking what he wanted?

'Aguandra's got political ambitions,' Jim Crabtree said softly, and Kingdom looked up to find the marshal's shrewd black eyes watching him. 'From deputy mayor all the way up to territorial governor.'

'That explains a lot,' Kingdom said pointedly. 'Between those two spreads there's a horse rancher called Isaac Haynes who ain't going to move without being pushed — but Aguandra can't be seen to be involved in violence.'

'So he acts cagey. Anybody watching — and there must've been plenty — all they know is he bought you a drink.'

'And as luck would have it, you're up for re-election.'

The cigar stopped halfway to Crabtree's open mouth. 'What the hell is that supposed to mean?'

'Come on, Crabtree, you're actin' like a parched coyote prowlin' around a poisoned water hole. An ambitious man's got a dirty job he wants doin', but his hands are tied. There's another man got a well paid job, enjoys polishing a badge, wants to stay in office. The ambitious man's already in a position to pull strings — but there's a price tag.'

'There ain't no tag — but if there was, it'd be more than my job is worth,' Crabtree growled, but his eyes had grown shifty, and Kingdom was unconvinced.

'There's just the two of us in this office,' Kingdom said softly, 'so if you want to make a proposition it's at least worth a try. Like you said, Marshal, anyone passing, all they know is you bought me a drink while doin' your duty and layin' down the law.'

'And if I tell you for the past five minutes you've been talkin' hogwash?'

'I can't argue,' Kingdom said, climbing out of the chair and turning towards the door. 'But I know of one sure way of finding out which one of us is on the right track.'

'Isaac Haynes?' Crabtree's boots hit the board floor with a thump. He leaned forward, planted his meaty hands flat on the desk and shook his head. 'Stay away from him, Hondo. The man was in the saloon, saw you talkin' to Aguandra. You ride up to High Plains he'll fix you with those yeller eyes of his and blast you out of the saddle with a Greener — always supposin' you get past his two sons and their goddamn Sharps Buffalos.'

'Hell, you just can't make up your mind what you want me to do, can you, Marshal?' Kingdom said, grinning.

'Get out of here,' Crabtree growled.

Kingdom was stepping out onto the stone steps when Crabtree called, 'You never did tell me your real name, Hondo.'

'That's right,' Boone Kingdom said, 'I didn't.' And, as he headed across the street towards the grandly named Majestic Hotel, he wondered if it had been Dave van Tinteren who had alerted the marshal to the earlier gunplay — and if it was, what else he had told him.

3

The willows were like grey ghosts alongside Coldwater Creek, the early morning mist a chill white blanket hanging over the river and the glistening wet grass.

But the sun was already well up. As she walked up the low rise from the new cabin, Helen Aguandra turned her face to its warming rays, took a deep breath of the clean air and raised both hands luxuriously to the nape of her neck to gather and lift her long dark hair and pin it high on the crown of her head.

It was a morning ritual that she relished: the walk to the river under the golden, early-morning light; the whisper of her feet through dew-soaked grass; the touch of pure, untainted air on her skin that was always the signal for her to lift her face to the endless skies, fix her hair, her blue eyes closed as her fingers worked nimbly and her face soaked up the sun's warmth.

Yet, always, the silent joy of each magical, dawning day that called her from the stuffiness of the cabin and directed her footsteps towards the low rise and the sight of soft grey willows of Coldwater Creek was swiftly banished.

Ric was up and dressed, out back shaving at the wooden bucket and in no hurry. Why should he be? They had no livestock. The forty acre patch where John Kingdom had raised wheat, oats and barley had returned to nature, and Ric had no plans to work it; had no plans to do anything, it seemed to Helen, but wait for instructions from his pa.

They were living on an abandoned homestead with no fixed boundaries. It was those unmarked limits and what lay beyond them to the west that obsessed Roberto Aguandra, and had led him to build the cabin for his son and send him there to live with his new wife.

That, and something else that Helen Aguandra — with a woman's perception — had observed in the senior Aguandra but could not define. Something more disturbing than a natural restlessness; almost its opposite; an eternal patience that masked something inside the man that was like . . . like what?

Not patience. Even there she was wrong, grasping for labels. Poison. Was that it? Something eating away inside the man . . . destroying him, and perhaps others around him.

And then the pointless, aimless musing was cut short as Helen Aguandra reached the top of the rise and was alongside the graves of John and Sarah Kingdom; the parents of the slim, earnest boy she had vowed one day to marry.

A sound came to her, carried on the still air. Her hand reached down absently to touch the damp wooden cross marking the woman's resting place, and she looked back through the light mists hanging below the west bluff and the dark pines, and watched a horseman approach.

★ ★ ★

Before reaching the Majestic Hotel, Boone Kingdom had changed direction and crossed the dark street at an angle to call on Dave van Tinteren. The visit had been short, and mainly for the purpose of borrowing a rifle. Kingdom figured that what the man had done for his father he could also do for the son; and besides, he wanted to ask a question.

The lawyer had been quite definite.

'As far as I'm aware, only two of us know about your past, Boone. Until you tell us different, that's the way it'll stay.'

So that was all right then — if van Tinteren could be trusted. From what he had said after that, it seemed that he could.

'I didn't get a chance to ask you what Roberto Aguandra wanted, Boone.'

'No,' Kingdom said, 'and I guess Ed Jaffe interrupted us before we got around to discussin' that fine woman I saw you with, Dave.'

Dave van Tinteren had laughed richly at that. 'All right, then let me fill you in. My guess is Roberto Aguandra was too damn cautious to come right out and say what he wants. But you were talking to Gus when I walked in — sure, I spotted those Remingtons from clear across the room — so you'd have been well primed before you got to that black hearted rancher and his no-good son.'

He'd grinned ruefully at Kingdom's raised eyebrows. 'I'm working for Isaac Haynes, Boone, so maybe I'm biased. But take it from me, Roberto Aguandra is the purest poison to have drifted out of New Mexico in the past ten years — and, since you asked, that fine woman you mentioned is Dawn Grey, just about the best thing that's happened to me in that same time.'

As Kingdom collected his blanket roll from Dusty Rhodes's stable, booked into the rooming house with the fancy name and climbed the narrow stairs to the room that offered a sagging bed, a flimsy chair, a cracked jug and wash bowl and not much else, he was recalling that ten years ago his pa had said to him, '*Son, Dave van Tinteren ain't white clear through — maybe that ain't possible, with a lawyer — but he sure as hell sticks with his clients like burrs to a cow's back.*'

That, Boone Kingdom reckoned, was just about the highest accolade a man could collect, and made Dave van Tinteren's stated allegiance a pretty good character reference for Isaac Haynes.

Kingdom slept well in the creaking bed, and rose early as was his custom. The sun was still below the eastern horizon, the high clouds streaked with tongues of flame when he collected the eager sorrel from a bleary-eyed Dusty Rhodes, buckled on the booted

Winchester he'd borrowed from van Tinteren then swung into the saddle and headed out of town.

He took the sorrel in a wide loop through the long grass and scattering of sage covering the lower slopes of the hill to the east of town, and after a mile picked up a broad cattle trail that headed in the right direction. The morning air was chill, its bite bringing tears to his eyes. He ducked his head, raised the pace to a steady canter, his mind already far ahead.

He'd told Dave van Tinteren he'd had a dream, but for a long time those dreams had been nightmares. No kid of fifteen, however tough, sees his family slaughtered without suffering from a mountain of grief. No vengeful boy wearing his pa's six-guns blasts three grown men out of their saddles and sleeps easy at night, undisturbed by the haunting of their dark and bleeding ghosts.

So the healing had taken time. His wanderings through the savage lands beyond Texas' western borders were signs of a boy growing to manhood without a clear idea of what he had done, or where he was going. From the time of the killings at Coldwater Creek he was aware that he had the gift of lightning fast reflexes. Before he was seventeen he had run ins with drunken white renegades who hankered after his guns and Mexican bandits who came looking for the gringo, *el niño de la sangre*. He was never bested, and his blazing six-guns brought him a growing reputation that dogged his back-trail and created the nuisance of weak men hoping to bask in his reflected glory, the menace of cheap killers confronting him in the dusty streets of shabby towns in a hopeless quest for instant fame.

The young Boone Kingdom had been forced by circumstances to follow a sad and violent trail to nowhere.

Well, Kingdom thought now, he was no longer young, that trail was long years in the past, and if the reputation had done anything worthwhile it had had given him the freedom of choice.

Three miles out of town, the rising sun now bright in his face, Kingdom sent his horse splashing through the shallow waters of a small stream that came gurgling down from the higher ground and would soon feed into Coldwater Creek. Here he pulled into a grove of live oaks, swung down from the saddle and spent time fashioning a cigarette while his horse bent its head to graze.

Hereabouts he had two options. His natural inclination was to keep heading roughly northeast, a course that would take him to the site of his old home. That inclination was fired partly by long-held feelings of guilt — he'd buried his ma and pa, then turned his back and ridden away — and partly by curiosity.

As he recalled it, he'd spent his first couple of years as an orphan raising seven kinds of hell in Sonora and Chihuahua before striking out for the

Bravo and working his way down to Laredo. It took him another year to ride north through Texas. A bloody gunfight against four hardened gunslingers in a town of the same name west of San Antonio got him christened the Hondo Kid. Six months later, eighteen years old and with too many unmarked notches on his gun, he was fighting for the Confederacy.

The Civil War had sobered many an intrinsically sensible man and left him looking ahead for a future in which violence would play no part, and Kingdom knew damn well it had left him a changed man. After Appomattox he had kidded himself he was wandering aimlessly, but though the long trail had taken all of two years it had led him inexorably north west, and a week ago he had crossed the Palo Duro.

He was returning to his roots. And last night he had told Dave van Tinteren he expected to find things exactly as they were.

Gut feeling overruled the head and convinced him he'd ride down that wide trail swooping past the rocky west bluff, emerge from the shadow of the tall pines with the cool breeze from Coldwater Creek in his nostrils — and in his mind he rode from there on in with an aching lump in his throat and the familiar scene blurred by tears and that didn't matter because, Lord, hadn't it all travelled with him, in his memory, for ten long years?

Angrily, Boone Kingdom dropped the cigarette into the grass and ground it under his heel.

Memories could lie, get overtaken by time. There was a new cabin below the rise at Coldwater Creek, a new man living there with his woman. Boone Kingdom's urge to see the old place had turned sour, yet he was sensible enough to know that to reject the idea entirely was wrong.

'Only one way to go about this,' he said softly, and a smile played about his lips as he walked over to the grazing sorrel. 'You brought me this far, old friend, so assumin' you're blessed with more sense than me, we'll do it your way.'

He found a stirrup, swung over leather and gently kneed the horse out of the trees, and with the reins hanging loose and his hands clasped on the horn he settled down to enjoy the ride.

It took the sorrel a few minutes to get used to the idea. Then it snorted joyously at the sudden feel of freedom, lifted its head to survey the terrain ahead, and stretched its legs into a fast, mile-eating gallop.

4

Seen from the western bluff, the new cabin's raw peeled logs glistened in the morning sun. On the dusty slope up out of the dip the pines still cast long shadows across the trail.

He eased his mount back, jogging in at an easy pace, knowing the sound of hooves would carry to Ric Aguandra. In the climate of unrest that prevailed over the land between the Rita Blanca and Coldwater Creeks, Roberto Aguandra's son would almost certainly emerge from the cabin carrying a gun, primed for trouble. But he would recognize his visitor and relax some, maybe even invite him to step down, though that, he considered with a wry smile, was unlikely.

If the girl was there . . .

He cast that thought out of his mind.

The horse dislodged a stone, sent it rolling. A woman laughed throatily, a warm, homely sound, and he cursed softly then lifted his elbows to wipe both sweating palms on his dusty vest just where it hung above the twin six-guns. He let his hands linger there, noted their faint trembling, for reassurance touched the six-guns' cold, hard butts and drew a deep, shaky breath.

Then he felt the horse's muscles begin working under him as it thrust up the sharp slope out of the dip. His own muscles knotted with tension. As they approached the cabin the aroma of fine cooking was in his nostrils and suddenly, as if in rebellion, his mouth went dry and he knew it was nerves and wondered, with a churning sickness in his stomach, if what he was about to do could in any way be justified.

Then the terrible misgivings evaporated and his mind settled into a blank coldness as a man appeared in the cabin's open doorway, stripped to the waist, the skin of his body a bleached white beneath the tan of his face and neck.

He was unarmed.

'What the hell do you want?' he growled, his eyes dark with suspicion.

Ric Aguandra was still poised like that, half in and half out of the cabin, his swarthy features fixed in a belligerent scowl, when without a hint of warning the visitor dipped his now rock steady hands to the twin six-guns in a blurring double draw of bewildering speed. Four shots rang out in the space of a single second. Four ugly, puckered holes were punched in the pale skin of Ric Aguandra's chest, grouped around his heart.

He reeled back, hit the door frame hard with his naked back. His eyes went wide with shocked disbelief. Blood spurted as his torn heart pumped valiantly in a prodigious effort to keep him upright. Then it stuttered, weakened. The strength drained from his muscles. He choked, slumped to his knees, fell forward across the threshold.

The woman's scream was a piercing shriek of horror that was a sharp knife plunged into ears still ringing with the echoes of gunfire.

He winced, felt the startled horse twitch beneath him, tightened his knees, muttered something, anything, his narrowed eyes fixed on the dimness beyond the open door.

Then a young woman flung herself out of the shadows. Her dark hair was wild, the thin cotton dress clinging to her body. Face streaked with tears, contorted with hate, she leaped into the doorway, stood with slender legs braced astride her dying husband. The Winchester gripped in white-knuckled hands swung towards him, blasted. He felt the wicked draught of the slug's passing and, with sadness, he gritted his teeth, lifted the six-gun in his right hand and shot her cleanly between the eyes.

She was thrown backwards as if kicked by a horse. The rifle clattered against the door frame, dropped onto the dead man's naked back with a dull slap. The woman twisted as she fell. Her bare feet, resting across his thighs, twitched, and were still.

He cleared his throat harshly, spat to rid his mouth of the reek of gunpowder. The tremor was back in hands that were clammy with sweat; his eyes darted, looking anywhere other than at the warm bodies streaked with bright, wet blood.

He glanced up at the grassy rise, thought he saw hazily outlined against the dazzling sun the shape of two wooden crosses, and frowned.

Then he planted his boots firmly in the stirrups, spun the horse away from the cabin in a swirl of dust and spurred it into a fast gallop that carried him past the rotting, fire-blackened timbers almost hidden by the undergrowth and once more onto the trail that led away past the high west bluff.

5

The high pitched, angry squealing of a horse coming to Boone Kingdom's ears was as welcome as the sound of clear spring water trickling over rocks. He dragged the back of his hand across his dry mouth and figured thankfully he was maybe ten minutes' ride away from something cold and liquid to ease his parched throat and refill his empty canteen.

Minutes later he topped a rise and squinted down on a wild swirl of activity, heard another shrill squeal followed by a bellow that could have been pain or anger and issued from the yellow dustcloud boiling over the corral that was set away from another smaller corral, a low, sprawling ranch house and the big barn with its adjacent bunkhouse. Beyond the spread, away to the north, thick groves of cottonwoods, willows and tall cedars covered the slopes that swept down to where the waters of Coldwater Creek gleamed like molten metal under the hot noon sun.

As he rode down the long slope, under the high crossbar of the gate and onto the spacious yard of High Plains, Isaac Haynes's thriving horse ranch, a tall man with a gaunt face streaked with sweat and dust was stepping out of the corral, ducking between the sun-bleached poles and straightening stiffly with a grimace of pain.

Behind him, a black mustang with rolling, white ringed eyes and glistening flanks, kicked its heels and galloped around the inside perimeter, mane streaming, tail flaring. The rawboned wrangler turned, glared at its antics for a couple of seconds then cuffed off his hat and threw it to the ground in disgust.

Another man emerged from the shadowy interior of the barn, walked over to the big tank alongside the windmill, scooped water and splashed it over his face and head then shook like a dog, showering sparkling droplets. Bareheaded, trail worn, he was as tall and spare as the wrangler, with the same broad shoulders and lean hips, the same black hair worn long.

Remembering Isaac Haynes, Kingdom guessed that he was looking at the horse rancher's two sons — and not a Sharps Buffalo anywhere to be seen. But Jim Crabtree's warning had also concerned Isaac Haynes and his fondness for a shotgun, and as he swung down alongside the corral and hitched the sorrel's reins to the top pole, Kingdom kept a wary eye cocked towards the house.

'A mean horse sure rattles the old bones some,' he remarked sympathetically, and the wrangler swung up and around from recovering his hat, raising fresh clouds of dust as he slapped it against his pants then rammed it on his head.

'Not mean. Don't like to be ridden

71

hard, any more than you would — and where the hell did you spring from anyway?'

'Yonder,' Kingdom said laconically, and jerked a thumb over his shoulder.

'Yeah? And now you're heading over yonder,' the wrangler said tersely, and also jerked his thumb, but in the opposite direction.

'That's inhospitable, Jake.'

The other man had strolled over. Black eyes glittered as water trickled from his lank hair down through sharp furrows in the lean face, dripped from the end of a sharp beak of a nose. He was drying his hands on the sides of his vest, and in the same unconscious movement they slid down over his bony hips, paused there for a moment, then fell to his sides.

'A man rides out to visit, least we can do is offer friendship,' he said, and his grin revealed flashing white teeth. 'You got a name, friend?'

'You shout Hondo, I'll know who you mean.'

'Ain't there a Kid tacked onto that?'

'Suit yourself.' Kingdom looked at the fixed grin, the glittering black eyes, the hands still lingering close to the naked hips. 'At that, you've got the advantage on me.'

'Always will have,' the man with the wet face said, and now there was a message in the black eyes. 'As long as you understand that, Hondo Kid, we'll get along fine.'

'Hell, pay him no heed,' the bruised wrangler said. He took a step closer, stuck out his hand. 'Jake Haynes. I guess that mustang shook all the good manners out of me. The feller carryin' the chip on his shoulder's my kid brother, Zeke.' He looked keenly at Kingdom, his eyes taking in the lithe, and tigerish, build, the low-slung twin Remingtons. 'What it is, you caught him off guard, Hondo. Zeke feels kinda naked without his guns, and after what Pa told us . . . '

'What your pa could've told you about me,' Kingdom said, 'would balance nice and easy on the head of a pin.'

'Well, he ranted for maybe an hour or more, jabbered so much most of his cold supper ended up back on his plate 'stead of in his belly.' Jake Haynes shook his head in disbelief. 'Carried on some more when he stomped out and took to his rockin' chair on the gallery. Smoked a last pipe gazin' up at the night skies like he wanted to shoot out every goddamn star, cursin' Roberto Aguandra all the way up an' down the Coldwater.'

'Message was, you hired up with Aguandra, some sort of two-gun straw boss gonna lead an army of 'breeds against Isaac Haynes and his rag tag crew.' Zeke Haynes grinned without humour. 'All that, on one, goddamn pin head.'

'Ah, hell, the man was usin' a figure of speech, Zeke.' Jake Haynes looked over at the now motionless black mustang, shook his head. 'Damn crazy horse,' he said softly, but there was grudging admiration in his voice and Kingdom warmed to the man. 'An' talkin of horses,' Jake continued, a sudden hardness in his voice, 'I ever see you run one down the way you just did, Zeke, I'll put you flat on your back.'

'I was in a hurry. A good rub down, he'll've forgot all about it by morning.' Zeke's black eyes were ugly. 'I've got a better memory, Brother Jake, stretches back a long way. The next time you threaten me'll be once too many. When you do, you better hope I ain't wearin' my guns.'

He swung on his heel and strode off across the yard, spattering the sun-baked yard with water as he headed for the barn.

'You two always at each other's throats?'

Jake spat. 'We ease off when the day of the week ain't got a Y in it.' He jerked his head. 'Come on. Pa's in the house doin' the books. He'll talk to you.'

'With the business end of a Greener?'

'That's Jim Crabtree shootin' his mouth off, I guess.' Jake Haynes, limping badly, squinted across at Kingdom as they neared the house. 'You know all about reputations, Hondo. Most of 'em're just loose talk sewn into one crazy patchwork of lies by men livin' empty lives.'

'Put it on display far enough from its origins and the lies begin to look like truth, Jake,' Kingdom said. Mexican spurs jingling, he followed the wrangler up the steps and onto the cool of the gallery, swept off his Stetson and walked past the old rocking chair and into the house.

Sunlight slanted through the windows. In the dazzling shafts of light sparkling dust motes floated lazily over a smooth board floor. Furniture was rich colonial, transported from back East. The room was a private museum to a way of life, the passage of a tough man's pioneering years on the frontier marked with reverence in the tintypes and trophies decorating the log walls.

Kingdom guessed that there would be half a dozen rooms in the sprawling ranch house. This one had the lived in feel that brings peace to a man's soul, leaves him unafraid of settling contentedly in one of the big, comfortable old chairs without first changing out of his dusty range clothes. Boone Kingdom knew nothing of Isaac Haynes, but if he'd wanted an insight into the man's character that went beyond Dave van Tinteren's unspoken recommendation, he could have come to no better place.

Jake Haynes limped across the creaking boards, said crisply, 'Visitor for you, Pa,' and went on through, closing the inner door behind him.

The man seated at the roll-top desk carried on writing, then put down his pen with a decisive snap and spun the swivel chair to face Kingdom.

'Life's just one damn surprise after another,' he said, and came loosely out of the chair, a tall man in his sixties moving with the grace of earlier years, his gaze critical but not openly unfriendly. Kingdom saw that Zeke had inherited the dark eyes, but none of their warmth and intelligence. Both younger men had taken their father's build, but still fell short in height and breadth.

Isaac Haynes stood now, hands on hips, challenging Kingdom.

'My departure from the saloon last night was hastened by an uncontrollable urge to change the general shape of Roberto Aguandra's face. You want to give him use of your guns, that's your business, but if you help him try to move in here, I'll kill you.' Without rancour, the tall horse rancher added, 'Is that what you're here for now?'

A long shadow fell across the room as Zeke Haynes walked in. Kingdom glanced around, saw him slouched just inside the doorway. A heavy gunbelt now encircled the man's lean hips, supporting twin Colts in tied-down holsters.

Then the inner door opened and Jake Haynes returned, freshened up, hair slicked back, and also wearing a heavy gunbelt. He pulled the door to behind him, leaned against it, his face faintly amused.

'Is this your way of setting up a talk?' Kingdom asked mildly, his eyes on Jake Haynes.

'A man with the reputation for being a gunslinger's good at his trade, or dead,' Isaac Haynes said bluntly. 'I talk on my terms. Your reputation outshines most others by the breadth of Texas, but my boys've got you tight pincered and I think that's something even you'd have trouble handling.'

Into Boone Kingdom's mind there flashed a picture of a young boy confronted by three ragged gunmen who thought him a kid still wet behind the ears but were already dead when they rode up past the dark pines. He recalled the Texas town of Hondo, a rain swept winter street with the light from the flickering oil lamps reflected

79

in the flooded ruts as two gunmen stalked him on either plankwalk then, without warning, threw down on a boy of seventeen who, they figured, was getting a mite too big for his worn-down boots. And he remembered four bodies lying in the mud, soaked by the driving rain, the flooded ruts running red with blood as he rode north along Hondo Creek, unscathed, and with a new name ringing in his ears that followed him to Waco and beyond and became the tag men used to refer to a kid who'd become a six-gun legend.

'How many times, how many towns, how many more stupid men?' Kingdom said, his voice edged with anger.

'I could end it right here,' Zeke Haynes boasted, 'if you're tired of living.'

'Back off, Zeke,' Isaac Haynes snapped. To Kingdom he said, 'Jake set up nothing, so what's all this nonsense about talk? Aguandra already gave me his ultimatum. Get off this land willing, or get run off. Only reason I can see for you bein' here is to enforce his words with those fancy Remingtons.'

'I'm beginnin' to wonder what the hell I *am* doin' here,' Kingdom said. He shook his head slowly. 'No, Haynes, you're wrong. I swapped half a dozen bitter words with Roberto Aguandra, a whole lot more with Crabtree and some a sight more friendly with David van Tinteren.'

'He's lyin',' Zeke Haynes said, and shifted his weight menacingly.

'Maybe not.' Isaac Haynes's dark eyes flashed angrily at his son. 'I heard some of those words, and they were a long way from friendly.' He looked keenly at Kingdom. 'Did Aguandra hire you?'

'You're the second man to ask that. The first offered the opinion that Aguandra wouldn't risk it, then looked like he was considering doing it for him but was too bashful to try.'

'Hah!' Isaac Haynes barked his contempt. 'That'd be Crabtree. Other name you mentioned is van Tinteren.

Where does he fit?'

'You'd need to look back more than ten years,' Kingdom said. 'Any books I read outside of school came from him. Any questions my pa couldn't answer were taken on by Dave.'

'Dave van Tinteren works for me,' Haynes said thoughtfully. He saw Kingdom's nod, seemed to come to a decision and stretched to his full height. 'You fellers've got more things to do than stand around playin' nursemaid to a cranky old man,' he said to his sons. 'Jake, that black devil in the corral needs rest and a few licks of embrocation a sight more'n you do. Let him alone until tomorrow.' Then his eyes darkened. 'You, Zeke, if you ain't too weighed down by that gunbelt then do something useful about the place 'stead of ridin' a good horse half to death for no damn reason.'

He stifled Zeke's angry retort with a cutting glance, watched both men tramp out onto the gallery and down the steps into the yard then nodded to

Kingdom and led the way through to a big kitchen with a scrubbed board table, tall oak dressers stacked with gleaming blue dishes, and a big, smoking-hot iron stove on which a coffee pot bubbled.

'I guess this is what I should have done in the first place,' he said, taking the pot and slopping scalding black coffee into tin cups and handing one to Kingdom. 'Roberto Aguandra's been a bad apple spreading poison across the Panhandle for too long. I can't continue to make that an excuse for my bad manners.'

He lifted his cup in a conciliatory toast to Kingdom, drank deeply then sat down on a wooden chair with an audible grunt that could have been age but was more likely caused by troubled thoughts. Indicating a second chair, he waited until the other man was seated then said, 'I settled here five years ago, called on Dave van Tinteren in his office when I was investigatin' existing claims to this land. There were none. Also, for the record, what went on between you and him before then has never been mentioned, and don't concern me.' He smiled crookedly. 'I seem to remember saying something about killing you. I'd like to think that was just me talkin' big.'

Boone Kingdom placed his hat on the table, and shook his head. 'No. A man defends to the death what's rightfully his, Haynes. Sounded like you were making a point to me, but I think you were saying it out loud to remind yourself. I knew a man once who'd do that: spend time over the supper table to state his commitment in words that gave comfort to his family and put steel into his soul so that, if the time ever came . . . '

'*As long as I've got breath in my body, the strength in my hand to pull a trigger,*' John Kingdom would say, '*I swear no matter who comes by here I'll keep you safe, both of you.*'

The unexpected recollection of his pa's exact words caught at his breath, but he knew that the time hadn't yet come to take Isaac Haynes into his confidence, and was uncomfortably aware from the horse rancher's steady, penetrating gaze that he might already have said too much.

'If Dave van Tinteren has confirmed that this place is rightfully yours,' he continued quickly, 'Jim Crabtree's forced by law to take your side in any dispute.'

'What dispute?' Isaac Haynes's eyes were amused. 'We're three years out of a civil war, country's still in turmoil and what Roberto Aguandra's doin' is bein' done by bushwhackers and jayhawkers all over Texas — an' he knows damn well I'm too proud to go crawlin' to Crabtree.'

Haynes paused. The amusement lurking in the intelligent dark eyes was stronger now as if, Kingdom thought, he was aware of the flaws in his thinking and was waiting to be challenged.

Boone Kingdom sipped his coffee, looked at the lean horse rancher over the rim of his cup and, on impulse, said, 'So why ain't he made his move?'

Haynes grinned his approval. 'You spoke to him. What was your impression?'

Kingdom frowned, thinking back. 'Full of his own importance. A hard man runnin' to fat, grown accustomed to success . . . ' He hesitated, remembering the way a deliberate insult had drawn no response, the curt nod to Crabtree as Aguandra rode down the lamplit street, the marshal's cautious probing. He put the cup on the table alongside his Stetson, ran a finger around the grey hat's brim, looked up and said slowly, 'A man greedy for land and high position, but without the — '

'Guts?' Haynes's head was dipped, his eyebrows up.

Kingdom shrugged. 'Could be. I was going to say without the ability to get either one of them on his own. Needs help from men in power. Never game enough to make a move unless he's damn near one hundred per cent certain of success.'

'Right. And both outfits — Rocking Z and this one — have got between six, eight men they can call on. That's cutting the odds too fine for Roberto Aguandra.'

'So if it's a stand off, and things ain't going to change — why not get on with your business instead of worrying about a vain man's impossible ambitions?'

Haynes's gaze had sharpened. 'Because what's inside Aguandra won't go away. Instinct tells me there's something more than greed behind what he's doing. Seems like he's a driven man, got a fire burning inside of him, says he must have High Plains — though Lord knows why.' He shrugged. 'But, that aside, things will change, Hondo, have changed already.'

'How so?'

Isaac Haynes pushed away from the table, refilled his cup, offered the battered pot to Kingdom who shook his head.

'I said upwards of eight men,' Haynes

said, still standing. 'How many have you seen?'

'You. Your two boys.'

'Rest of 'em's up in the hills. All the stock I had's sold. So I figured it was time they were out combin' the brush for the wild herds, leavin' this place protected by . . . ' — a horse's hooves rattled in the yard and Haynes dipped his head towards the sound — '. . . protected by Jake out there, and Zeke, and my faithful old Greener.'

Kingdom nodded. 'So Aguandra'd know that, and maybe figure he was as close as he'd ever get to his one hundred per cent sure thing.'

'Well, that's the way I had it read,' Isaac Haynes said, and he glanced towards the open door as footsteps pounded the gallery then advanced across the big room. 'I'd reckoned on Aguandra makin' his try, calculated that three of us could handle most anything he threw at us, get this finished once and for all. Until last night, that is, when a feller called the Hondo Kid rode in and looked set to tip the balance too far in Aguandra's favour — '

He broke off, flipped his hand in greeting and said, 'Hi, Jim, grab yourself a coffee,' and Kingdom turned to see Marshal Jim Crabtree, sweat-soaked, coated with trail dust and with a hard glitter in his eyes.

'Isaac.'

Crabtree crossed to the stove, poured coffee into a cup, drank deep, then let out an explosive breath.

'Goddamn, I needed that.' He jerked his head at Kingdom and said, 'How long's he been here?'

'Hour. Maybe more, maybe less.'

'What did he look like?'

Haynes frowned. 'What the hell's that supposed to mean?'

'For Christ's sake. Isaac!' Crabtree slammed the cup on the table, slopping coffee. 'Right now he's sittin' at your table drinkin' your java, but if I'm right he rode here from the old Kingdom spread and I want to know what the hell impression you got when he rode in.'

'Funny,' Boone Kingdom mused aloud, 'but I don't recall leavin' the room.'

'Huh?'

'I was born with a tongue, Crabtree. Why ask Haynes all this?'

'Aw, to hell with it!' With a smooth movement that belied his bulk. Crabtree whipped out his 45, held it loosely pointing at Kingdom's belly.

'There's an old trapper name of Ike Moss, comes by maybe once every couple of years,' he said harshly. 'Rode in today, mid-morning, told me he come down past the Kingdom spread, found Ric Aguandra and his wife both dead, shot down like rabid dogs in the doorway of that new log cabin.'

'Jesus!' Isaac Haynes breathed. He slumped into his chair and went still and silent, his eyes unfocused.

'I rode straight here,' Kingdom said. 'Ain't no one can verify that — but why would I kill Aguandra?'

'Because you've got the best possible motive,' Crabtree said. 'Dusty Rhodes poured half a bottle of Gus's whiskey down his gullet and started shoutin' how your real name's Boone Kingdom, and you're back to reclaim your home.'

'All right, I'm Kingdom,' Boone Kingdom acknowledged. 'But the rest is something Dusty got out of that bottle.'

'You'll have plenty of time to argue the point. I'm takin' you in for murder.'

'No, Marshal.' Boone Kingdom shook his head, and his lips twisted in a sad smile. 'You've got the drop on me, but that's never been enough. I'd kill you while the message was crawlin' from your brain to your trigger finger. You'd die, and never see me move.'

'I don't doubt you could do that,' Crabtree admitted.

And as Isaac Haynes resurfaced from wherever his thoughts had taken him and his eyes focused, then widened in shock at what they saw, Jim Crabtree lifted an eyebrow and something hard and heavy crashed down on the back of Boone Kingdom's head and the room exploded in a flash of blinding light that left him blind and deaf and he felt himself falling sideways out of the chair and then felt nothing . . .

6

Before he opened his eyes he could taste blood in his mouth. He tried to lift his hands and felt the burn of rawhide on his wrists, knew that they were tightly bound and secured to the pommel. Then his horse stepped in a hole, his teeth clicked, and he knew the reason for the blood: while unconscious, he had bitten his tongue.

Feeling sour bile rising in his throat, Kingdom tried to spit from a dry mouth, felt a thin trail of spittle on his chin and turned his head to wipe it against his raised shoulder. His eyes scraped open. He blinked painfully, blearily in the bright sunlight, eased his weight forward in the saddle and at once realized his ankles were lashed together by a rope under the sorrel's belly.

Memory returned, and with it a

headache that was a hot iron spike jabbing at the tender core of his brain in time with the pounding hooves. Someone had swung a pistol butt at the back of his head, Kingdom decided with a flicker of anger. That would have been cold-eyed, black-hearted Zeke Haynes, sneaking up behind him, seen by his pa who had registered shock but was too late snapping out of his reverie.

And what was the reason for that spell of wool-gathering? Ric Aguandra's death left the old Kingdom spread empty, removed even the flimsiest justification for Roberto Aguandra's takeover of Isaac Haynes's High Plains. Or had Haynes been looking ahead with numb dismay, seeing Aguandra galvanized into action with half the Rocking Z crew moved east, trapping him in what he would probably call a tight pincer?

Ah, hell, he was doing too much thinking, too soon. His head ached like a rotten tooth, thoughts full of importance were small birds fluttering, evading capture with ease. He squeezed his eyes shut, sucked in several deep breaths; opened his eyes again to look far ahead across the green and gold of the undulating prairie to where West Fork's buildings poked their roofs and square false fronts into the afternoon's shimmering haze.

Either accidentally, or with cold deliberation, Zeke Haynes had struck dangerously hard. To make haste with his prisoner Crabtree had cut across open country, but to be this close to town meant there was an hour's hard riding behind them. That was a long time for a man to be unconscious, and posed another question Kingdom was too dazed to answer.

Did Zeke Haynes want him out of the way because he might throw in his hand with Roberto Aguandra — or was there a deeper, more personal reason? The most likely answer, Kingdom decided numbly, was a bit of both. Zeke had struck hard because it was in his nature to be vicious. But the six-guns at his hips suggested that it was also in his nature to be vainglorious, and the heady route to notoriety for such a man would mean a show-down with the gunslinger they called the Hondo Kid . . .

A taut trail rope led from Kingdom's sorrel to Jim Crabtree's horse. The marshal was leading the way at a fast canter, his high-stepping mount kicking up dust that clogged Boone Kingdom's nostrils and collected like grains of coarse sand under his eyelids.

He used what movement he had in his feet to kick the sorrel, and jounced clumsily up alongside Crabtree. The stocky marshal flicked a glance sideways, wordlessly hauled in the trail rope, spat out a brown stream of tobacco juice then registered his disinclination for conversation by clamping his jaw and deliberately facing front.

That was fine by Boone Kingdom. He rode stirrup with the marshal for the remaining miles, clear of the choking dust-cloud but unable to do a damn thing about the agony in his head that had him swaying and hanging onto the horn as he clenched his teeth to hold back the churning nausea in his belly.

They rode together up the centre of West Fork's main street with the sun still high enough to cast razor-sharp shadows across the rutted thorough-fare, drawing no curious glances because at that time of day the sight of two men on horseback was as commonplace as ticks on a coyote.

Crabtree swung down outside the stone jail-house. He hitched both horses to the rail, then took a folding knife out of his pocket, pulled open the blade and swiftly sliced through Kingdom's bonds.

His charity went no further. He unfastened a saddle-bag, took out Kingdom's rolled gunbelt, then turned impassively to watch as his prisoner slid out of the saddle onto quivering legs and slumped forward to rest his head on the saddle. A big fist pulled a bunch of keys out of the same pocket that held the knife, and Crabtree climbed the steps and unlocked the door.

Face still pressed against smooth saddle leather, eyes closed, throat moving convulsively, Kingdom extended his arms stiffly across the patient sorrel and flexed his fingers as returning circulation brought with it fresh agony.

'All right, let's move,' Crabtree growled.

'Hell, you're all compassion,' Kingdom said huskily.

'Was that what was in your mind when you gunned down those helpless kids?'

'In case you're interested, the man who did that's still out there,' Kingdom said.

He pushed away from the horse, took a breath, then walked unsteadily up the stone steps and brushed past Crabtree into the office.

'Straight through,' Crabtree said, plucking a big bunch of keys from a peg and dangling the heavy ring from his finger.

Despite the discomfort he was suffering, amusement flickered in Kingdom as he passed through the inner door. Only last night he'd sat in the chair in front of the desk, drunk fine whiskey with a man who'd been only a playing-card's thickness away from downright fawning. Now he was tramping through to a different world, a cold, stone cell-room of high barred windows and twelve-by-twelve strap-steel cages.

He stood to one side as a cell door was unlocked, caught the stale, musty smell of the jail mingled with the marshal's rank sweat, then stepped inside and heard the door shut with a grating clang.

'Last thing I ate was a strip of jerky for break-fast,' he said, sitting down gingerly on the wall bunk and removing his Stetson. 'I guess you feed prisoners?'

'In good time,' Crabtree said. He glanced back, hesitated with what

Kingdom could only call a troubled look on his face, then went out, slamming the door.

A clump of hair on the back of Kingdom's head was matted with dried blood. He pressed the patch with the tips of his fingers, felt swelling and sponginess beneath the stiff hairs and winced as pain knifed through his skull and bright lights flashed behind his eyes. Knowing it was impossible to lie down, he sat with his back against the wall and his head well clear, pulled his legs up onto the bunk and crossed them, then patted his shirt and pulled out a crumpled sack of Bull Durham.

Well, he'd sure got himself into a fine mess.

He began fashioning a cigarette, then grimaced as he saw the puffed flesh encircling his wrists and full realization hit him. So much for a gunslinger's reputation. Hell, he'd been felled by a blow from behind, hog-tied when he'd been in no shape to resist, sat astride his horse, then thrown into jail — and all on the say-so of a trapper who was probably halfway crazy with loneliness.

No, that was unfair, Kingdom admitted, and wrong anyway. The trapper had done his duty in reporting the murders. Any blame for his imprisonment lay with Marshal Jim Crabtree, who had listened to an arthritic old hostler filled to over-flowing with Gus's strong liquor, jumped to a conclusion so obvious it had blinded him to all others, and ridden out to make his arrest.

But what other conclusions were there?

Kingdom dug a match out of his pocket, struck it on the edge of the bunk, fired up the cigarette and blew a stream of smoke towards the bars.

Well, he mused, narrowing his eyes against the smoke and contemplating the glowing end of the cigarette, even allowing for a brain that was too scrambled to think straight, there didn't appear to be many that would hold water. And if there were, a man coming up for re-election would still plump for the most obvious suspect in order to please the voters, then worry about the rights and wrongs of it when his man was behind bars.

That inclination would be even stronger when the victims were close kin to a man who himself was seeking high office. A case of mutual back scratching, Kingdom decided wryly. No powerful man ever made it to the top without treading on toes, without callously squashing a few small fry; the benefits to be gained from catching a big fish were guaranteed to influence a weaker man's judgement.

Thoughts were batted back and forth, with no obvious answer poking its head up and screaming for attention. The quirly slowly burned down. Boone Kingdom's eyes drooped. He trickled smoke, the cigarette dangling from his lips, his chin on his chest. In that comfortable dreamlike zone halfway between sleep and wakefulness, he felt a smile twitch his lips as an imp of the perverse whispered that most of the blame lay with his sorrel horse, who'd led him all the way across Texas to High Plains.

But the twitch of amusement was his undoing. The cigarette fell from his lips and dropped down his open shirt front, he came fully awake with a yelp as hot ash seared tender skin, and he was up on his feet, half naked and slapping the remains of the cigarette into shreds when the cell-room door banged open.

'Visitor,' Jim Crabtree called.

He reached up to light the lamp hanging from a hook in the cell-room's ceiling and, as Kingdom shrugged back into his shirt and vest and realized most of the afternoon had passed him by, the rangy figure of Harry Gregg loomed behind the marshal.

The cell door was unlocked and Gregg stepped inside.

'This could be elk, buffalo — or just plain dog,' he said, handing over a steaming bowl of meat stew. 'But

I've drunk enough of Crabtree's coffee to know what this is, without openly recommending it.' He placed a tin cup on the floor alongside the bunk and turned to the marshal.

'I'll holler when I'm through, Jim,' he said, and Crabtree nodded, locked the cell door and returned to his office.

'So,' Boone Kingdom mumbled around a mouthful of meat. 'I kill Roberto Aguandra's son, his foreman comes to visit. Or maybe to gloat.'

Gregg leaned against the bars. His craggy face was sober, his eyes pale mirrors reflecting the last of the day's light. The sweeping dragoon moustache drooped over a mouth set in a thin, hard line.

'I told you a reputation don't make you immortal,' he said. 'Now you're locked up, for another man's crime.'

'If I didn't do it,' Kingdom said, 'what am I doin' in jail?'

'Crabtree has to please Karl Tanner, who's scared you'll rob his bank.

Aguandra's boy's dead. Crabtree's always been in his pocket, and wants to keep his badge.'

'I'd worked that out.' Kingdom clattered the empty bowl onto the floor, picked up the coffee, took a sip. 'Who's this other man whose crime I'm paying for?'

'A man who was sparkin' Helen Sloane before she up and changed her name to Aguandra, and has been talkin' of killin' her new husband ever since.'

'Helen Sloane,' Boone Kingdom said softly. Dave van Tinteren's words came to him and he remembered a slip of a girl with long pigtails who had sat by him in a sun-drenched schoolroom smelling of warm dust and chalk, a girl whose books he had carried across a scented summer meadow and who had looked up with huge, soulful blue eyes and made a solemn promise to marry him when they grew up.

'If all this is common knowledge, what's happenin' to me is a set up.

So what the hell are you here for, Gregg?'

Harry Gregg's laugh was a harsh, ugly sound. He pushed away from the bars, paced across the cell to place a hand on the stone wall and stare out of the narrow, barred window. The sounds and smells of the town drifted in on the eddies of cooling air. Kingdom stared past the foreman at high evening skies streaked with crimson, listened to the crack of a muleskinner's whip and the sound of many hooves, the hollow stamp of footsteps on the plankwalk, the bang of a door.

Then, as if with a difficult decision made, Gregg swung around.

'There's still a way out, if you'll take it,' he said. 'One last chance, if you like, before I paint you a grim picture. It's this: open your mouth now, tell me you'll side with Aguandra against Isaac Haynes, and when I walk out of here, you go with me.'

Without hesitation, Kingdom shook

his head. 'I know less about Aguandra than he knows about me, but I'd as soon go to bed with a rattlesnake.'

'Then listen. Today, after months when it seemed nothing'd go right for Roberto Aguandra, you rode out of town and suddenly everything socked neatly into place. He's sent me to present his thanks, Kingdom — and to tell you that when the time's right he, personally, is going to take great pleasure in killing you.'

'The last bit makes sense,' Boone Kingdom said. 'The rest went over my head too fast to follow.'

Gregg perched on the edge of the bunk, located the makings in his vest pocket and began fashioning a cigarette.

'Two things happened while you were out of town, both of them in the Breaker saloon. First was, old Dusty Rhodes let slip your real name. Second was, that old trapper, Ike Moss, came bouncing up the street on his half-blind old mule with news of the double killing.'

A match flared as Gregg fired up his quirly. He sent the match hissing onto the tin plate, sucked a lungful of smoke, coughed, and said, 'But I guess Jim Crabtree already told you that.'

'By hell, you're a circumambulatory bastard!' Kingdom said, and as Harry Gregg gaped in amazement with the cigarette halfway to his mouth, he said, 'You're wanderin' around in circles like a drunk with one leg shorter'n the other. Get to the point, Gregg.'

The big foreman grinned. 'Naw, you've got it all worked out. With you out of the way Aguandra can be certain you ain't takin' sides, and move in on Haynes. While he's takin' care of that chore, you're bein' kept nice and cosy for when he's ready to walk in and plug you.'

Kingdom nodded impatiently. 'With Ric dead, I can understand why he'd want to do that. But for a man with ambitions for public office the easy way, the safe way, is to set tight, wait for me to hang for murder.'

'Yeah, but you're just not understanding at all,' Harry Gregg said, his voice heavy with scorn. 'You see, Kingdom, Roberto Aguandra wantin' to kill you never did have anything to do with the murder of his kid.'

7

It seemed to Boone Kingdom, as he thoughtfully sipped the strong coffee while Roberto Aguandra's foreman sat bowed forward on the bunk with the cigarette smouldering under his big moustache, that this moment in the strap-steel cell in West Fork's jail was what his life had been leading up to for the past, oh, twelve months or more; from the time, in fact, when he'd deliberately let the reins hang slack for the first time and his big sorrel had turned his nose towards the rich grass-lands of the Texas Panhandle.

But believing that, and understanding what was going on, were two thoughts separated by a gulf as wide as the Bravo was long.

Hell, it was bound to happen, sooner or later. His back-trail snaked a couple of thousand miles and ten years into his past. Somewhere along it his smoking six-guns had left a man stricken with a tearing grief that tormented his soul and refused to heal. But to prise one name out of memories dulled by the thunder of blazing guns, blurred by gunsmoke drifting across the dusty streets of nigh on a hundred frontier towns, was surely an impossible task.

'Don't even try askin' me,' Harry Gregg said, anticipating the unspoken question, his pale eyes cynical as he came up off the bunk and bent to crush the cigarette on the tin plate. 'Aguandra's a mean bastard with something black weighin' heavy on his mind. After twelve months on the Rocking Z, I'm no closer than you to knowin' what that is. I mostly do what I'm told, collect my pay at the end of the month — '

'Mostly?' Kingdom cut in bitterly. He put the empty cup on the floor, stood up quickly to confront the foreman and said, 'Does that mean you pick and choose those jobs that suit you? If so, what's your yardstick, Gregg? Is it how much profit, or how far the wrong side of the law? Where does drivin' a decent horse-rancher off his spread come into your sense of right and wrong?'

'That question ain't arisen,' Harry Gregg said easily. His big hand planted itself against Kingdom's chest and pushed him back a step. 'You want good advice, Kingdom, don't waste energy makin' decisions unless something's right there bangin' you in the face.'

Light and shade swept across his square countenance as the office door clicked open and the oil lamp swung in the sudden draught. Dave van Tinteren walked into the cell-room, dark-suited, pants tucked into glossy riding boots, wearing a stiff-brimmed black Stetson and with the keys to the cells jingling in his hand.

Harry Gregg laughed, and moved away from Boone Kingdom. 'Dave, you taken on the job of deputy?'

'Crabtree's over at Gus's grabbing a bite to eat. I guess he trusts me.' The lawyer winked at Kingdom, unlocked the door and swung it open. As the big straw boss walked out, van Tinteren said, 'Give Aguandra a message for me, Harry?'

'Shoot.'

'Tell him that today, history repeated itself.'

'That supposed to ruin his sleep?'

'Depends on his conscience. But in any case it should set him thinking.'

He clapped the big foreman on the shoulder, watched him saunter out, then stepped into the cell.

'You sunk to statin' the obvious?' Boone Kingdom enquired, one eyebrow raised.

'Forget that,' Dave van Tinteren said brusquely. There was the faint sheen of sweat on his forehead. His thick, greying, dark hair was untidy, and he ran his fingers through it almost absently. 'We'll give Harry Gregg a couple of minutes, then the two of us are walking out of here.'

Boone Kingdom frowned. 'No, I

can't let you do that. You've built a career and a reputation. You help a prisoner break out of jail, that's all gone, you're finished in West Fork.'

'Reputation?' Dave van Tinteren's laugh was hollow. 'Are you telling me the value of a reputation, Hondo Kid? Listen,' he said, 'a reputation is inside the man as well as in the eye of the beholder; there're more ways than one it can be ripped to shreds. Better to be finished in the eyes of the world for righting a wrong, than to be dead in my soul for letting an old friend die for a crime he didn't commit.' There was a hint of embarrassment in his eyes but a square, no nonsense set to his jaw as he stated bluntly, 'I could defend you in a court of law, Boone, but long before the case is tried Roberto Aguandra will gun you down.'

Kingdom picked up his Stetson and put it on, feeling stunned by the lawyer's fervour; the man's passion was almost physical, yet he could see no good reason for it.

'Crabtree strikes me as weak, not bad,' he protested half-heartedly. 'Surely he'd stop short of allowing cold-blooded murder?'

'Jim Crabtree would have no choice. You've got to understand the depth of Aguandra's fury, Boone. To get at you he'll kill, and kill again. If necessary he'll buy drinks all round in the Breaker, raise a drunken lynch-mob to storm the jail. That's why I'm getting you out of here — so, come on, let's move.'

He took hold of Kingdom's arm, urged him out of the strap-steel cage. Together they crossed the lamplit cell-room to the office door. There, van Tinteren held up a restraining hand, opened the door a crack and slipped through the narrow opening.

Seconds later he was back, carrying Kingdom's gunbelt. With the door pulled to behind him he waited as the twin Remingtons were buckled around the slim waist, the thongs lashed to the lean thighs.

'All right,' he said quietly. 'The only difficult part's crossing the street into the alley. Maybe twenty yards. Stick close to me. Anybody passing will recognize my dark suit, be reassured that nothing's wrong.'

He grinned at Kingdom's quick look, and said, 'Yeah, OK, so I admit a reputation has some uses.' Then he opened the door for the second time and led the way through into Jim Crabtree's office.

The marshal's presence was so strong in the room, Boone Kingdom shivered. On the big desk a cigarette still smouldered in the cow's-hoof ashtray filled with blackened stubs. The open bottle and empty glass added their raw whiskey smell to that of strong tobacco. It was as if the lawman had walked out, leaving an essential part of him behind.

Dave van Tinteren opened the street door with care, peered out, then called Kingdom forward. They left the office quickly but without rushing, went down the steps and walked across the street like two men done with business for the day, apparently making for Dusty Rhodes's livery barn that was almost directly opposite the Breaker saloon.

Signs swung, creaking, in the light breeze. There was the smell of rain in the air. A waddie was swinging up into the saddle outside the bright lights of the saloon. Another man was standing back in the shadows, unseen but for the glow of his cigarette.

Then Kingdom and van Tinteren were across the street. The lawyer cast a lingering glance towards his locked office, then ducked into the narrow alley and broke into a jog.

A few feet behind him, Kingdom saw the man in the shadows outside the saloon move to the edge of the plankwalk as the mounted waddie rode away, thought he saw the flash of pale skin as a face was turned his way.

Then the edge of the building cut the man from view. Spurs jingling, Kingdom ran the length of the alley after van Tinteren. Out in the open again he swung sharp right and saw the lawyer some twenty yards ahead, running fast up a wider back alley that curved to rejoin the main street.

He caught up with a sharp burst of speed. Breathlessly, he said, 'There could be trouble,' and saw van Tinteren's vigorous shake of the head and knew that what had seemed like a snap decision by the lawyer was a carefully planned break.

But the best laid plans can't anticipate the unexpected.

The open rear entrance to Rhodes's livery barn loomed. Kingdom heard a horse nicker, a gruff voice uttering calm words. Then he was smiling in the gloom as he saw the old hostler hanging on to a cheek strap, struggling to hold the big sorrel which had caught Kingdom's scent.

Alongside the sorrel, a wiry little red roan was saddled and waiting.

Kingdom reached out, gripped van Tinteren's shoulder.

'I hadn't thought this through,' he said quietly. 'After what you've done, there's no way you can stay here, is there?'

'Boone, there's no damn time for small talk,' the lawyer said roughly.

He took hold of the red roan's bridle, found a stirrup and stepped up into the saddle, quickly swung the horse's head towards the back alley and kneed it out under the stars.

'Me and my big mouth,' Dusty Rhodes mumbled. 'Hell, I'm sorry Boone. I'd already run off at the mouth before Ike Moss rode in, didn't see no harm, and I guess I've always been kinda proud of what you done all those years ago . . .'

As Kingdom took the sorrel's reins from the hostler he saw the abject misery in the old man's eyes and said swiftly, 'Forget it, Dusty. With my record this would've happened anyway.'

He planted both hands on the horn, glanced down as his foot fumbled for a stirrup, and was stopped with his leg in the air as a voice rasped from higher up the dark runway.

'Hold it right there, Hondo!'

Kingdom lifted his head slowly. His boot slipped into the stirrup. He kept his hands still.

Behind him, there was the scrape of hooves on packed earth as Dave van Tinteren edged his horse into the shadows against the back wall.

Ed Jaffe stepped past an empty stall, stopped. His legs were spread, his pistols holstered, his hat jerked down low over his mean, glittering eyes.

'So that was you, over by the saloon,' Kingdom said.

'You saved me some trouble. I knew Crabtree was in the Breaker. You hadn't come out the jail, I'd've gone in after you.'

'Yeah, you and half the town,' Kingdom said, and felt Dusty Rhodes shift alongside him, out of the corner of his eye caught the glint of metal.

'Even the Hondo Kid can't shoot

through a goddamn sorrel gelding,' Ed Jaffe jeered.

'Don't need to,' Dusty Rhodes growled. He stepped away from the sorrel. There was a double-barrelled shotgun in his hands. 'Back off, Jaffe, before I blow you into the next county.'

With a muttered curse, Ed Jaffe went for his gun.

But he was no Hondo Kid. His draw was slick and fast, but all West Fork's old hostler had to do was move a finger.

Dusty Rhodes squeezed both triggers at the same time. The blast of two heavy cartridges packed with gunpowder and shot was like the roar of a cannon. For a fraction of a second the dazzling, twin muzzle flashes were sheet lightning illuminating the interior of the barn.

The aching void that followed was silent and dark.

Ed Jaffe had been blown off his feet. The numbing quiet was broken by the clatter of his falling six-gun, a drawn-out groan that was the agony of a man dying, the wet slithering as he slid down the wooden side of the empty stall. The powerful double blast at close range had ripped through his middle, carrying his torn entrails through his shattered backbone, almost cutting him in half.

'Move, Boone!' van Tinteren yelled. 'We'll have the whole town down on our heads.'

But Boone Kingdom was already in the saddle.

The shocking explosion almost under its nose had sent the sorrel squealing and rearing in terror. With his hands still clamped on the horn Kingdom braced his arms and used the powerful upward surge to carry him off the ground. The horse's front hooves pawed the air, then slammed down. Kingdom lithely swung a leg over the saddle, flung his arms around the muscular neck then hauled on the reins and dragged the big animal around. Gritting his teeth, he used the sharp Mexican spurs to send the horse lunging out through the wide doors.

Dave van Tinteren was already at the end of the curving back alley, a bent shape atop the fast-moving roan, starkly outlined against the lights of West Fork's main street. Kingdom's sorrel swiftly ate up the ground, came out into the lights closing fast on the lawyer's smaller horse.

Behind them, as they raced towards the edge of town, a pistol cracked and voices roared in outrage.

Then they were clear, the last of the buildings falling behind, their horses' hooves drumming on the hard-packed earth of the rutted trail. Half a mile out of town Dave van Tinteren swung north away from the high east ridge and they streaked across open grassland, their only light a fitful moon that floated from behind the high, drifting clouds.

8

The furious pace set by Dave van Tinteren across the undulating, open prairie left Boone Kingdom no option but to clench his teeth, blank his mind to the pain in his head that had now diminished to a dull, nagging ache, and pray that the big sorrel didn't step into a hole.

In ten years of exile, memories fade. On that broad expanse landmarks were few and distant, and difficult to pick out by the patchy, intermittent moonlight. As far as Kingdom could judge, they were on a line that would bring them to a point midway between his old home and High Plains, the Haynes spread. In memory, nothing lay in that area but a clear stretch of Coldwater Creek and beyond that the last strip of northern Texas before the section of Indian Territory to the west of the

Cherokee Outlet.

Several times, van Tinteren looked over his shoulder. Once he yelled, 'No sign of them so far,' the words whipped away like leaves in the wind, and with a heady feeling close to exhilaration Kingdom thought, no, and if they're coming they ain't going to catch us at this rate.

As the miles were eaten up by the galloping hooves, the gallant red roan's head began to bob and, gradually, it fell back to the powerful sorrel. Kingdom drew alongside and called, 'We'd best ease up,' and the pace was slackened to a fast canter.

'Dave, you got this all worked out?'

'Remember that sweeping bend in Coldwater, a mile east of your pa's old spread? We cross there it'll look as if you're getting out, heading northeast through the Nations to Kansas.'

'But I'm not?'

Dave van Tinteren flashed a grin. 'Along that bend the water's not deep. We get two-thirds of the way across, we can turn west and ride through the shallows for almost two miles.'

'Won't fool 'em, Dave.'

'It'll buy time.'

After that they rode in silence. The stiffening breeze had banished the earlier threat of rain, driving the clouds towards the New Mexico border so that the still rising moon was a bright disc floating in clear skies. When they topped a low rise, the curve of Coldwater Creek was a glittering sabre blade cutting through the grassland, the willows lining its banks silver grey in the moonlight.

Then the weary horses were carrying them down the long slope to the water. Low down, the breeze was barely noticeable, the chill rising knee high as they neared the creek's banks, with a promise of mist to come. The willows whispered as their shoulders brushed through the low branches and they rode straight over the soft edge and crunched onto a flat expanse of wet shale, then splashed into the creek and drove the horses across at a high-kneed trot.

Here, Coldwater Creek was no more than forty yards wide. After thirty of those, van Tinteren turned the red roan towards the west, again forcing the pace and maintaining that ten yards from the far bank.

The waters were flat and sluggish, the moon directly above now so that they rode along a thin, glittering pathway that was thrashed into a fine rain of sparkling jewels by the flashing hooves. Refreshed by the cold waters, the horses snorted and tossed their heads. Even Dave van Tinteren's tense mood was broken, and he laughed out loud as his stiff-brimmed Stetson was whipped off to hang by its chin strap across his broad shoulders.

They came out of Coldwater Creek when the moon had slipped behind a solitary cloud whose broad shadow flitted eerily across the land to cloak them in darkness. The terrain was rougher on this side of the river, the trail narrow and snaking, the going difficult in the gloom. Gradually the timber thickened. They began to climb, the horses blowing, the riders easing their weight forward in the saddle.

'Getting close, now,' van Tinteren said.

'Not before time.'

The lawyer's laugh was warm. 'A man like you, a ride like this should be old hat.'

'I'm a tired old man at twenty-five,' Kingdom said, grinning in the darkness.

Then van Tinteren lifted an arm and, as they veered off the trail that was now little more than a tortuous deer track and the cloud floated away to let the pale light of the moon wash over the hillside, Kingdom saw the outlines of a low shack that was like a pile of blackened logs poking through thick undergrowth.

'Ike Moss's cabin,' Dave van Tinteren said, sliding out of the saddle. 'A good place to rest and talk.'

* * *

'I guess I've got the wrong picture of this old feller,' Kingdom said.

They were sitting by the light of a guttering candle in a room no bigger than the strap-steel cell. But the grumbling, pot-bellied stove was emitting waves of heat, chairs draped with thick Navajo blankets were set close together on a dirt floor covered with sleek animal skins; log walls were impossible to see behind the clutter of traps, snow-shoes, faded tintypes, stiff leather harness and stuffed elk heads with gleaming eyes — all hanging from nails or wooden pegs — and the single bunk and the square table set under the window were littered with clothes or tin plates and cups, but spotlessly clean.

'You had him figured as a filthy old devil, slept with his flea-bitten mule?' van Tinteren said. He was sprawled in one of the chairs, jacket off and draped over the back, his face flushed with the heat, his eyelids drooping

129

comfortably after the meal of beans and fried jerky.

'Something like that. I heard he was away most of the time, so I expected something run-down, wide open, stinking of wolf or coyote.'

'He leaves the door unlocked, a good stock of provisions there to be used. But there's an unwritten rule: leave the place as found, or expect Ike to come looking for you with his old Henry.'

Kingdom was stretched full length on the bunk's cornhusk mattress, using a pile of buckskins and pelts as a high pillow.

'History repeats itself,' he mused. 'So, ten years ago, it was old Ike discovered where I'd buried my folks, reported me missing.'

'Nine years ago. He was up in Montana for a year, came back and solved a mystery.'

'Mystery?' Kingdom frowned, then nodded. 'Yeah, I can see that. Someone eventually must have rode out from town — Clem from the mercantile with supplies, maybe old Dusty stoppin' by to chew the fat with Pa — but it must have caused some speculation finding the cabin burned down, two graves up on the rise, me nowhere to be found and three bodies lyin' rotting — '

'No bodies, Boone.'

'The hell you say!'

'Nope. Ike saw your folks gunned down, stayed until he was damn sure you were safe. But that's all he saw. Dusty was first man out there after the killing, found it pretty well like you said. Two graves. Plenty of horse sign. A lot of blood soaked into the ground. But no bodies.'

'All right,' Boone Kingdom said tightly, 'if the bodies had been spirited away, how does anyone know they ever existed? Where the hell did those stories about me gunnin' down three killers spring from?'

For a long minute there was a pleasurable silence in the cabin. The stove hissed gently. A coyote howled somewhere way out in the hills. One of the horses nickered, and Kingdom knew instinctively it was the big sorrel.

Dave van Tinteren shifted his weight in the chair, shook his head. 'I guess nobody ever asked that question before,' he said ruefully. 'As I recall, the story about your prowess with a pistol started circulating round about the time old Ike Moss rode down from Montana. Maybe everyone assumed he saw what you did. His story got told a hundred times, bits chopped off, other bits stuck on.'

Kingdom chuckled. 'Well, at least I had a guardian angel for part of the time out there. Maybe it was old Ike's mystic influence made me stay back in the woods.' He slid his hand up his chest, felt the bulge of his tobacco sack and said softly, 'And then, ten years on, he finds another man and woman shot down . . .'

'Sure. But when I said history repeated itself, that's not what I meant, Boone.'

Puzzled, Kingdom tilted his eyes down, peered along his legs and across his boots at van Tinteren, waited patiently for enlightenment.

After several moments' silence, the lawyer sighed. 'Ike didn't find the bodies of Aguandra and his wife. He got there sooner than he let on, watched them die.' He gestured helplessly. 'Leave it, Boone. Think about now. I brought you out here because when you rode up West Fork's main street you took people's minds off more important things.' He gestured apologetically. 'I'm not saying Jim Crabtree has trouble handling two thoughts at the same time, but continual harassment by Roberto Aguandra had already muddied his thinking. With you out of the picture, Jim can collect his thoughts, do what has to be done.'

'Seems to me what has to be done is the capture of a runaway killer called the Hondo Kid, and the feller who betrayed a trust by casually walking him out of a jail cell.'

'That's not so, Boone, and you know it.'

The lawyer heaved himself out of the chair, his white shirt gleaming as he picked up the coffee pot from the stone hearth, shook it then banged it on the glowing stove. As it immediately began to sing, he looked hard at Kingdom.

'We know you didn't kill Aguandra. So who did?'

Kingdom pursed his lips, again patted his vest pocket for his tobacco, let his hand slide away. 'Harry Gregg hinted, but wasn't much help. But, hell, I reckon I've seen enough. A feller with his horse plumb wrung-out from being ridden too hard, built like a gunslinger but swaggerin' out of a big barn with his hips naked. An older feller who gets the stuffin' knocked clean out of him when Crabtree rides up to report the killing . . . '

'So what Jim Crabtree will do,' van Tinteren suggested quietly, 'is thank me for getting him out of an awkward spot, and turn up at High Plains early tomorrow to arrest Zeke Haynes.'

'That wasn't in your mind when we lit out of West Fork. As I recall, you looked over your shoulder more than once.'

'You never can be sure which way a man will jump. But as time passed, with no sign of Jim Crabtree snapping at our heels with a posse, I got a clear picture of him in his office, that whiskey bottle close to hand as he shifted his thoughts around into their correct pigeon holes.'

'Nevertheless,' Kingdom said, 'arresting Zeke Haynes will be one tough task.' He sat up, swung his legs off the bunk, watched van Tinteren put two tin cups together on the table and pour in scalding black coffee from the bubbling pot. 'Or will Crabtree have help?'

'We'll be there,' the lawyer said, and handed a steaming cup to Kingdom, his face expressionless. He dropped into the chair and said, 'Ever since Roberto Aguandra approached you in the Breaker, you've known deep down you'd take the other side.'

'Could be risky, ridin' into High Plains as bold as brass. Isaac Haynes'd be within his rights gunnin' down an escaped prisoner. Also, you could be wrong about Crabtree. A sensible man might look hard at the night skies and wait until daybreak to raise a posse.'

'And give you as much as eight hours' start?' The lawyer shook his head. 'No, Boone. I know Jim Crabtree. The man who's been threatening to kill Ric Aguandra as good as wrote a signed confession. That's the man Crabtree will be hunting.'

Perched on the edge of the bunk, Boone Kingdom sipped the hot coffee, felt the wound on his scalp contract with the movement of his jaws as he swallowed, and thought critically about the man who'd wielded the six-gun with such skullbreaking force.

Yes, Zeke Haynes was the rotten apple in the High Plains' barrel. If it had been in Kingdom's mind all along to help Isaac Haynes, Zeke's presence might have poisoned his thinking and made him turn away. But with Zeke locked up for murder, that left two honest, hard-working horse ranchers up against half-a-dozen armed men. With an enraged Roberto Aguandra whipping up passions and using his son's spilled blood as a justification for driving the family out of the Panhandle, Isaac and Jake Haynes would need to keep their eyes skinned for riders with blazing six-guns coming at them out of the dawn mists, or the terrible sight of torches flaming in the dark night.

And what about Dave van Tinteren? Could a lawyer past his best years, more familiar with pen and paper and the power of the spoken word than the skills of gunplay, be of any use against a determined strike by trail-hardened waddies?

A smile twitched Kingdom's lips as more wise words surfaced from his past, and he heard his father saying, '*Dave came from back East, son, with clean fingernails and a classy education. But he's the kind of feller can knock a man down with one clean punch, and I ain't yet seen a finer shot with six-gun or rifle.'*

For the first time, Boone Kingdom noticed that Dave van Tinteren had a gunbelt holding a Colt Navy .36 strapped about his thickening waist. A man in middle age, no family, not yet settled.

'Funny name for a saloon,' Kingdom said thoughtfully. 'Breaker . . . '

Dave van Tinteren laughed softly. 'The full title is heart breaker. It describes the fine woman who runs the place better than any man could, because that's what a feller will discover to his cost if he tries to court the lovely Dawn Grey. Somehow it didn't seem appropriate for a tough cow-town, so at my suggestion it got shortened.'

'And your heart never got broke?'

'I guess I don't take much notice of signs, Boone.'

'And run roughshod over rules and

regulations — which I suppose is my way of saying thanks for what you did today, Dave.'

'Then don't. I was a close friend of your family, Boone. I watched you grow up, so seeing you again is reward enough. But you're not yet out of the woods, by a long chalk. Your reputation clings like a burr. Marshal Jim Crabtree's made a damn fool of himself, so now he's got two reasons for wanting you gone from West Fork. And if you have a hand in stopping Roberto Aguandra's takeover of High Plains, that'll double his reasons for wanting to plug you full of holes.'

'About which,' Kingdom said, 'I've been having some thoughts.' He put the tin cup on the floor, and this time his fngers made it all the way into his pocket and brought out his tobacco sack. As he began to fashion a cigarette, he said, 'Crabtree told me Aguandra arrived on the scene maybe nine years ago.'

'From New Mexico.' The lawyer

nodded. 'Isaac Haynes had been here six months or so.'

'It was renegades from over the border killed my folks.'

'You exacted a terrible revenge, Boone. That would appear to even the score.'

'But you never can be sure which way a man'll jump,' Kingdom said, and his grin was mocking in the bright flare of the match as van Tinteren recognized the echo of his own words and smiled crookedly.

'Get some sleep, Boone,' he said tiredly.

He reached for the candle, pinched out the flame, and Kingdom heard the chair creak as the lawyer stretched out for the night.

As he lay back on old Ike Moss's bunk, the cigarette glowing in the dark, the smell of hot wax in his nostrils, Boone Kingdom pondered on the reasons why a man would nurture savage thoughts of hatred and vengeance when, as Dave van Tinteren had pointed out, rough justice had been done.

If he was right, and Roberto Aguandra was in some way connected with the Kingdom killings, then looking in the reverse direction might offer a clue.

So, Kingdom mused, what feelings did he hold for Roberto Aguandra?

The question, he decided, sucking on the cigarette and trickling smoke into the darkness, had no answer, because he was comparing unlikes. Aguandra's only crime was — maybe — to be kin to three killers. He had gunned down Aguandra's relatives in cold blood.

And yet . . .

Ten years *was* a long time. Even if Kingdom's return had reopened old wounds, common sense said a rancher with political ambitions would look at the consequences, and stop short of murder.

Unless, Kingdom thought sleepily, there was something else. And that thought wouldn't go away. Aguandra's involvement in the killings must have been deeper; there was a link — something Kingdom didn't know or couldn't know — that explained why a prosperous rancher was prepared to risk a career to kill.

'*Today*,' van Tinteren had said, '*history repeated itself*,' — whatever the hell that meant!

And then, as weariness settled over Boone Kingdom like a heavy blanket and his eyelids began to droop, he remembered where his cigarette had finished up the last time this had happened, plucked it from his lips and flicked it, sparking, into the stone hearth, and wearily closed his eyes.

Tomorrow, he'd tackle Dave van Tinteren.

9

There seemed to be nothing stirring when Boone Kingdom and Dave van Tinteren rode under the high crosspiece of the gate and onto High Plains. The sun was still low in the east, chasing their long shadows before them across the packed earth but not yet warming the crisp air. Mist hung over the creek. A thin column of white smoke rose from the ranch-house's stone chimney.

'Three, four miles away,' Kingdom said, referring to the lone horseman they had seen from the high ground. 'No posse, so it looks like you were right. But if he's takin' his time, could be twenty minutes before he gets here — if it is Crabtree.'

'A lot of ifs, but who else could it be,' the lawyer said, 'at this time of day, heading in this direction?'

'Well, looks like he'll have to make

his arrest in Zeke's bedroom.'

Even as Kingdom said the words, Jake Haynes came around the barn atop the gleaming black mustang that only yesterday he had been reviling with strong words and admiring with experienced eyes. He glanced across at the two horsemen, then headed over to the corral and leaned down to grasp the single gate bar. With the pole in one hand and the reins in the other, he neatly backed the horse, then nudged it forward through the opening and dropped the bar into place.

'Now that,' Kingdom said loudly, 'is just plain showing off,' and as his voice rang out in the still air and Jake Haynes flashed a cool grin, Isaac Haynes walked out of the house to the edge of the sun-drenched gallery, stretched both arms up to touch the low, overhanging eaves with his fingers, then relaxed and stood watching through narrowed eyes, hands on hips.

'One to come,' van Tinteren said quietly.

'And ten minutes to do it — if he ain't already lit out,' Kingdom said. Van Tinteren flashed him a glance, swore, then swung down from the red roan.

Kingdom also stepped out of the saddle, and both men hitched their mounts to a pole then wandered around the corral to where Jake was off-saddling the black.

Boone Kingdom was uneasy. They had talked nothing through, over a breakfast cooked and eaten mostly in silence. That silence had extended through clearing up, securing the cabin and saddling the horses, and had been broken only by desultory snatches of conversation as they headed down from the high timber through the cold light of dawn.

The only clear thought they carried with them from the previous night's conversation was the intention to be there at High Plains when Crabtree arrived. That they had achieved, but in some ways it put them in an impossible situation, in other ways one bordering on the dangerous.

Dave van Tinteren was Isaac Haynes's lawyer. Kingdom and van Tinteren were there, Kingdom supposed somewhat hazily, to discuss how to handle the Aguandra threat — but if things got tough they could also be siding with Jim Crabtree in the arrest of Isaac Haynes's younger son.

However, before they got around to any of that they were likely to be confronted by Isaac Haynes and the hot-tempered Zeke. Isaac had looked shocked when his son loomed behind Boone Kingdom with a six-gun raised to strike. In the time between Kingdom toppling from the chair and being hoisted unconscious onto his sorrel, the horse-rancher had ample time to talk to Jim Crabtree and correct the situation. That he hadn't done so suggested he had no intention of surrendering his son to the law.

Well, Kingdom thought wryly, what little time there was left was trickling away like dry sand down a gopher hole. Crabtree could be no more than a few minutes away, and for some reason Isaac had disappeared into the house.

'I guess you know your job,' Kingdom said, as Jake Haynes finished with the black and came over to the rails, lugging his saddle.

'Some mustangs make it easy,' the wrangler said tightly.

Catching the hostile tone, Kingdom laughed. 'If not easy, worthwhile when the fighting's all finished.'

Jake Haynes reached up to hang the saddle over the top pole, sleeved the sweat out of his eyes, then climbed out of the corral and turned to drag the saddle down with him. As he slung it over his shoulder and headed for the barn, he said, 'I admire your nerve, Hondo, but I advise you to cast your mind back, recall what Jim Crabtree told you about Pa.'

'You ask brother Zeke why he near rode that horse to death yesterday?' Kingdom called after him.

'Leave him be,' van Tinteren said, as Jake walked on in a stony silence. 'And what's this about Isaac?'

'Oh, I guess Jake was referrin' to his pa's likin' for a shotgun — and if I'm not mistaken, that's what he's totin' now.'

Isaac Haynes was back on the gallery, and now came clattering down the steps and started across the yard towards them. The tall horse rancher had his Stetson rammed down on his head, a plug of tobacco bulged in one lean cheek, and he carried a sawn-off American Arms 12-gauge in the crook of his arm.

'You got any ideas?'

'Yeah,' Kingdom said sharply. 'Keep out of this, Dave.'

As the lawyer began a terse objection, Kingdom held him firmly back with one hand and strode to meet Isaac Haynes.

The two men met in the centre of the yard, came to a standstill separated by six feet of dry dirt that was like an invisible wall of antagonism.

'That's far enough,' Isaac Haynes snapped. 'I want you to know that what happened yesterday in my house had nothing to do with me, ain't my way. But the law took you in, so you've either broke out yourself, or been sprung by a good lawyer.' His eyes drifted to van Tinteren, then back to Kingdom. They were questioning but uncompromising. The shotgun had lifted to point at Kingdom's belt buckle.

'Almost right,' Kingdom said. 'What happened was I was broke out of jail by the man standing behind me — and you know damn well he had good reason, Haynes.'

'Dave always has his reasons,' Haynes said. His dark eyes were suddenly guarded, but in their depths something close to fear stirred as he asked. 'Are you telling me there's justification for setting you free?'

'Where's Zeke, Haynes?'

'Zeke's gone. Rode out not long after Crabtree took you to town, ain't been here all night. But that's not your concern. I don't know why the hell you turned up here, but you're on the run and it's my duty to turn you in.'

'Even if I'm innocent of any crime?'

'That's for the law to decide.' The man's big-knuckled hands jerked the shotgun, and Haynes said, 'Unbuckle your gunbelt Kingdom, let it fall, or this scatter-gun'll cut you into two bloody pieces.'

'You're not fast enough to back up that threat, Haynes,' Boone Kingdom said, 'and by the time you get to be fast enough you'll be too damn old to lift a gun.'

Haynes spat a dark stream of tobacco juice, flashed white teeth in a grin. 'Hell, hard talk comes cheap. You think I'd go up against the Hondo Kid without back-up — ?'

'Rider comin'!'

The loud holler came from the barn. Kingdom swung round, saw Jake Haynes step out into bright sunlight with a long rifle held across his chest;

caught the muffled beat of hooves and looked over towards the gate to see a rider cutting at an angle across the grassy slope, heading for High Plains.

'Jim Crabtree,' Isaac Haynes said, as a badge flashed in the sunlight. 'Your horse is way over at the corral, a rifle and a shotgun got you pinned. With the marshal comin' through the gate there ain't nowhere for you to go, Kingdom, so act sensible, stay put, maybe we'll get this thing settled.'

Crabtree brought his horse under the high crosspiece at a fast trot, his blue eyes sweeping the yard, taking in the two men standing stiff and tense in the middle but lingering the longest on Jake Haynes lounging in the doorway of the barn with his buffalo gun. As he drew near to Kingdom and Haynes he reined in, slid heavily from the saddle and left the reins trailing.

'You've got one hell of a nerve,' he growled, walking up to Kingdom. 'More nerve than sense, or you'd be fifty miles away and still running. And you, Dave,' he fumed, rounding on van Tinteren, 'what the hell d'you think you're playing at?'

'Making sure there's no miscarriage of justice,' the lawyer said, strolling up to join the group. 'Too often proves fatal.'

'Goddamn!' The marshal dragged off his bandanna, mopped his neck and face and shoved it in his pocket. He slapped at his clothing, raising clouds of dust, then turned and spat. When he lifted his head he was glaring at Isaac Haynes.

'You know why I'm here?'

'A prisoner bust out of your jail. You've found him, and the man who aided and abetted. The law says you take them in.' The horse-rancher's dark eyes glinted. 'Or maybe not. If I've got it wrong, you'll tell me.'

'Jesus, this is one helluva thing.'

Haynes smiled crookedly. 'And that sun's getting a mite hot. Why don't we all go in the house?'

Crabtree hesitated. Then his jaw

muscles bunched, his blue eyes took on a hard sheen. 'Where's Zeke, Isaac?'

'I don't know — and that's the truth.'

'You hear what he's been shoutin' about these past weeks?'

'He shouts loudest when he's in his own home, Jim.'

Crabtree took a deep breath, let it out explosively. 'All right. Tell Jake to put up that buff' gun, look after my horse. Maybe we can all get together, talk this through civilized while I wash the dust out of my throat.'

Without waiting for a reply he spat out his tobacco plug and brushed between Kingdom and Haynes, swept the shotgun to one side with a stiff arm and stalked off towards the house.

His words had drifted to Jake Haynes, who stood the long rifle against the barn. Kingdom turned to the marshal's lathered horse, looped the loose reins around the horn and smacked the dozing animal on the flank. It jumped, tossed its head, then trotted down the slight slope towards the wrangler.

'So far, so good,' Dave van Tinteren said quietly.

'Well, it's goin' the way you said it would,' Kingdom admitted as they walked towards the house, 'but with Zeke Haynes on the loose I'm as nervous as a kitten down a well.'

Crabtree had gone straight through the living-room to the big kitchen. When Kingdom and van Tinteren tramped through, Isaac Haynes was already slopping hot coffee into four tin cups. That done he slammed the pot back on the stove.

'Set,' he said tightly. 'All of you.'

Chairs scraped. Haynes remained standing, his back stiff.

Knows what's coming, Kingdom thought, dragging out the makings. Been going mechanically through all the right motions like a law-abiding citizen, all nice and cosy inside a big set of blinkers. But now that's past. Crabtree's going to brand his younger son a cold-blooded killer, ram the painful truth down his throat in his own house.

'All right,' Isaac Haynes gritted. 'Let's get on with it.'

Crabtree shook his head. 'First, let's clear the air some.'

He took a battered cigar out of his shirt pocket, accepted the match Kingdom proffered, snapped it into flame and within seconds was enveloped in a cloud of acrid blue smoke. Grinning sheepishly at his contradictory actions, he took the cigar beteen thumb and fingers and jabbed it at Kingdom.

'I was wrong to arrest you, feller — but that seems to be a habit I've got into. Isaac, I've also been wrong listenin' to Roberto Aguandra's tough talk and doin' not a darn thing about it. That's over. Finished.'

'That's the best news I've had all day,' Haynes said with deep irony, 'but it don't change much.'

As Kingdom fired up his cigarette and stowed away the tobacco sack he knew Haynes was right. Crabtree could apologize and bluster and maybe state emphatically that now he'd seen the error of his ways he'd ensure that the law was enforced in West Fork — but that's all it was, bluster. His recent record of abject bootlicking and freeloading showed he would never be strong enough to outface a man like Roberto Aguandra.

Crabtree shook his head impatiently at Haynes's words. 'Now to Zeke — and let's cut out the bullshit. Zeke gunned down Ric Aguandra and his wife, plugged the both of them in the doorway of their home. You know it, I know it.' He squinted shrewdly at Haynes. 'But you say he's not here?'

'If he was, he'd've met you with guns blazing,' Haynes said bitterly, and Dave van Tinteren nodded agreement.

'That's clear enough, so let's move on, Jim,' he said.

The marshal glared, not yet over his grievance at the way the lawyer had helped Boone Kingdom.

'All right,' he said. 'If Zeke ain't

here, I can't arrest him. But you know it's inevitable, sooner or later, he pays for what he done . . . '

'For God's sake, Jim!' Haynes breathed.

Crabtree frowned, jammed the cigar into the corner of his mouth.

'All right,' he said for a second time. 'Last night, Roberto Aguandra was in my office. And you had it figured right, Isaac. Sending your boys into the hills has convinced Aguandra now's the time to make his move.'

He shifted the cigar around his mouth, then took it it out and looked at the wet end with distaste.

'How long?'

'Twenty four hours.' He squinted at Haynes. 'You've got one day, Isaac.'

'From when?' van Tinteren asked with a lawyer's attention to detail.

'Who the hell knows?' Crabtree said. 'Take it from last night — eight o'clock, maybe.'

The back door clicked open, hinges creaking as Jake Haynes came in. He shut the door, settled with his back against it, his eyes narrowing as Jim Crabtree glanced at him, then went on.

'All I know,' the marshal said gruffly, 'is when the time's up, Aguandra and his crew'll hit you when you ain't expectin' it — and with just the two of you against that bunch, you'll be in worse trouble than the Cheyenne was four years ago at Sand Creek.'

10

'Isaac, you've been here, what, eight or nine years?'

Dave van Tinteren's words cut through a silence that was as thick as the smoke from Jim Crabtree's cigar, snapped tension that was as tight as wet rawhide.

Jake Haynes cursed softly, pushed away from the back door and crossed to the stove to pour coffee.

'Thereabouts,' Isaac Haynes said, in answer to the lawyer's question. 'But that don't mean a thing, because you and me both know I got no official claim to this place.'

'Forget the law. What about Aguandra?'

'On the Rocking Z? Same time, I guess,' Jim Crabtree said, squinting through the smoke. 'Maybe a year less than Isaac.'

'All right. So why now? Why,

after something like eight years, does Aguandra decide he wants High Plains?'

Boone Kingdom nodded as van Tinteren echoed his own thoughts. 'I'd wondered about that. Only reason I could come up with was he took time to get established before makin' a move.'

'But that's the way a sensible man would operate.' The lawyer shook his head firmly. 'A sensible man would wait, but he would never make his move just when he's embarking on a career in politics.'

'And he wouldn't shoot his mouth off about murderin' a man just rode into town — but that's what he's a-doin',' Jim Crabtree pointed out.

'Exactly!' There was suppressed excitement in van Tinteren's voice. 'He's doing that because he's got a reason. But what's his reason for moving against High Plains now, with never a hint of it in the past eight years?'

'You baitin' us so you can come up with the answer, Dave?' Isaac Haynes asked. 'And what's this reason for wantin' Kingdom dead?'

'No, to your first question. I'm as baffled as you are. And the reason for wanting Boone Kingdom dead . . . well, that's part conjecture, part gossip . . .' He spread his hands as if in bafflement, and Kingdom allowed himself a thin smile.

Knows more than he's letting on, knows more than anybody in West Fork, he mused. But why was he holding back, playing his cards close to his chest, acting the crafty lawyer and sidestepping awkward questions? There was no conjecture, not on his part, only facts. And talk of gossip was his way of publicly debunking the stories that had come from Ike Moss — though no old-timer Kingdom had come across ever opened his mouth unless he was sure of his facts.

As van Tinteren absently began picking at a thumbnail, Jake Haynes said thoughtfully, 'Ain't nothing changed here at High Plains to set a fire under Aguandra's tail. We trap the wild herds, break mustangs, sell trained horses to the military and whoever else needs 'em. Cut timber in the woods for buildin' and such like. Head for town for relaxation at weekends . . . ' He shrugged. 'We're happy just the way we are.'

'Jake's right,' Isaac Haynes said. 'I buried my wife on this spread, built a life for me and my two sons, so all this jabberin' bein' tossed back and forth is time wasted. The whys and the wherefores ain't stoppin' Aguandra. Let's cut the talk and look at some facts. Jim, you must have come out here with some ideas in your head. Let's have them.'

'Zeke, first,' Jake said, watching the marshal. 'You goin' after him?'

Jim Crabtree, took a breath, pushed his lips forward, his blue eyes troubled. 'Not in any way you'd notice.' He dropped his eyes and flicked ash from the cigar, then looked directly at Isaac Haynes. 'Last night, Aguandra did most of the talkin', because I let him. Thinkin' about that ruined my sleep. But what come out of that tossin' and turnin' was the notion that I should ride out to the Rockin' Z, try to talk him round.'

'The man's driven by some devil we can't reach,' van Tinteren said. 'It's more time wasted.'

'And Zeke?'

Still looking at Isaac Haynes, Crabtree said slowly, 'I keep my eyes skinned, Isaac. Tackle him in the unlikely event he crosses my trail. Otherwise . . . '

Haynes nodded, smiling faintly at the clear message in the marshal's blue eyes. 'That's fair enough. All of it. You can't do more than talk to Aguandra. And if Zeke shows up here . . . ' He shot a glance at Jake, and as their eyes locked he said softly, for Jim Crabtree's benefit, 'If he shows up here, one way or another we'll get him down to West Fork so you can lock him up for murder.'

Into the eerie silence that was like

a pall hanging over the warm kitchen, Boone Kingdom said, 'Haynes, it looks like Roberto Aguandra's got scores to settle with both you and me — and neither one of us knows what the hell's goin' on. Easiest way of findin' out is to confront him. Right now I'm headin' for town, but when word comes Aguandra's on the move, I'll be back here to stand alongside you and Jake — if that's OK with you?'

'Hell, I'd be a fool to turn down an offer like that from the Hondo Kid,' Isaac Haynes said wryly and, as Kingdom came out of his chair, the rancher stepped away from the stove and the two men sealed the bargain with a firm handshake.

Jim Crabtree climbed to his feet, stubbed out the cigar, and turned towards the door. As he also rose, Dave van Tinteren said, 'No call for you to leave, Boone. If Aguandra moves quickly you could be caught cold.'

'There's an old-timer got something to say to me,' Kingdom said, and van

Tinteren nodded.

'Yeah, I thought that'd be it.'

Crabtree had gone, and already they could hear the sound of his horse. Dave van Tinteren flipped a finger to Isaac Haynes, and Kingdom followed the lawyer out of the kitchen and through the living room to the gallery. The sun was high now, the shadows deeper under the overhang, the light on the yard dazzling. Dust still drifted from the marshal's departure, and Kingdom sniffed the air, thinking of the long day, the longer night to come.

Jake Haynes brushed by and down the steps, called, 'See you later, Hondo,' and headed for the barn.

Behind them, Isaac Haynes said tersely, 'Nine years I've bin here. If Roberto Aguandra thinks he can wrest this place off me because of some crazy notion he's got pickin' away at his brains, he'd best think again.'

'He'll come at night, the moon at his back,' Boone Kingdom said, 'enforcin' his crazy ideas with his

men's blazin' six-guns.' He laughed.
'You ain't movin', and I don't aim
to die. Whichever way you look at
it, there's goin' to be one hell of a
fight.'

11

Boone Kingdom and Dave van Tinteren followed Jim Crabtree's example and took the short route into town, cutting across country in the heat of the day, their horses kicking up a drifting dustcloud that mingled with the heat-haze dancing and shimmering all around them, forever out of reach.

They swung their mounts into West Fork at a tired canter, van Tinteren heading on through town to tether his horse at the hitch rail outside his office and attend to neglected business.

Boone Kingdom stopped at Dusty Rhodes's livery barn, slipping from the saddle into the cool, rustling straw to remove the rig from the lathered sorrel and hang it on a rail.

'Took most of this morning to clean the place up,' the old hostler said gleefully. 'There was bits of Ed Jaffe stuck to every goddam board in the place, most likely be comin' across some I missed from now till Christmas.' Then the grey eyes became shrewd. 'I guess you give Crabtree the slip, eh, Boone?'

'You could say,' Kingdom said, his tone noncommittal. 'I think he's still out there, Dusty, chasing his shadow across the prairie.'

He clapped the hostler on the shoulder, then left him, still chuckling as he limped down the runway leading the big sorrel, and strode across the street towards the Breaker.

A quick glance up and down the street revealed nothing out of the ordinary. Some way past Jim Crabtree's office a heavy freight rig was grinding towards the mercantile, pulled by a six-mule span. Several men were about, but Kingdom judged them to be ranch hands or nesters in town for supplies, to get horses shod, equipment repaired, or to take care of any of the countless small, irksome tasks vital to the running of their businesses.

Of hard-eyed, armed punchers of the kind Aguandra would have on his payroll there was no sign, but as Kingdom crossed the plankwalk and pushed through the swing doors he told himself the absence of hired gunslingers was to be expected; when the rancher made his move it would be sudden and direct, following the course of Coldwater Creek from the Rocking Z, not by way of West Fork.

It was now just past midday, and the saloon was almost empty. A drummer in green derby hat and a fancy jacket was sitting at a window table smoking a corn-cob pipe and cheating at solitaire. At the end of the bar a thin man in a dark suit who could have been a bank clerk was staring moodily into a glass of beer. Sunlight slanted almost vertically through the windows onto the stained sawdust, and the smell of stale beer was more noticeable because of the absence of cigarette smoke and sweating bodies.

Kingdom murmured 'Howdy', then spent time at the bar rolling a cigarette. As he lit up and breathed out the first twin jets of smoke, the lanky figure of Gus appeared from a room out back.

'I guess I should report you to the management.' Kingdom said, 'but I'm just too darn tired.'

Gus grinned. 'Just as well. Management was in there with me, goin' through the books.'

He tipped a jug, slid the glass of beer along the counter in its own pool, watched Kingdom stop it deftly, lift it to his parched lips and drain it in one long draught.

Kingdom put down the empty, sighing his satisfaction.

'So what does management say about me leading her man along the shady paths of outlawry?'

'Says the first beer's on the house, but don't read nothing into that.' Gus winked. 'I think she's buying information.'

'About Dave breakin' me out of

jail? There's nothing to tell, Gus. Jim Crabtree was in the wrong, knows he ain't got a legal leg to stand on. Right now he's on his way to the Rocking Z, goin' to try to talk sense into Aguandra.'

Another full glass slid across the bar as Gus pulled a face. 'And you, Hondo, how'd you fare at High Plains?' He chuckled. 'Naw, it's Boone Kingdom, right? I guess I'd better get used to that new name of yours.'

'Old name,' Kingdom corrected, sipping the fresh beer then taking a deep pull at the cigarette. 'I got apologized to by Isaac, then recruited myself into the defence of his spread — should I be needed. And now *I'll* buy some information, Gus,' he added, trickling smoke. 'Tell me, how long before old Ike Moss comes in for his first snort?'

'Oh,' Gus said, squinting his eyes and gazing airily up at the rafters, 'in about twelve months' time, if he sticks to old habits. If he don't — two years!'

'Goddamn!'

The curse was explosive, and along at the end of the bar the morose bank clerk jumped so hard he slopped beer across the counter. Gus wandered over that way with his cloth, did the necessary swabbing and reached for the jug to provide a refill.

Thoughtfully, Kingdom turned and leaned with his back to the bar, idly watching the traffic in the street.

'When did he ride out, Gus?'

'Before I rolled out of bed, that's for sure.'

'You a confidant of his?'

'Meaning what?'

Kingdom looked down at his cigarette, frowned. 'I'm talkin' about eight or nine years ago. I'm pretty certain the old cuss saw something when my folks were killed — but the only person he's told is Dave van Tinteren.'

Gus came back over, wiping the length of the bar with the damp cloth.

'Well, I ain't no confidant. But you were there yourself, Boone. What Ike saw, you must've seen too.'

Kingdom sighed, shook his head. 'I was a kid, petrified, hiding in the woods on the wrong side of a rise . . . .'

He winced as a wagon rumbled past, one dry bearing squealing enough to set teeth on edge. Across the room the drummer caught his eye, lifted the pack of cards, riffled the edges and called. 'Care for a game, my friend?'

'Not now,' Kingdom said absently. Suddenly tense, his eyes were looking beyond the drummer, fixed on a tall figure heading at an angle across the street from the Majestic Hotel.

'Forgot to tell you,' Gus murmured at his shoulder. 'Zeke Haynes rode in late last night.'

'Yeah, I sorta figured he might be here,' Boone Kingdom drawled, 'with Jim Crabtree set on wastin' a full day out there along the Coldwater.'

And then boots hammered on the plankwalk, the swing doors were thrust back with a crash and Zeke Haynes slammed into the Breaker. His greasy black hair stuck out all ways from beneath his dusty black Stetson. He wore the crumpled clothes of a man who had spent a night sleeping rough. But the twin Colts glinted wickedly at his lean hips, and their shine was matched by the ugly glitter in his wild black eyes.

'Trail's end, Hondo,' he gritted.

'For you,' Kingdom said easily. 'You put a rope around your own neck when you murdered Aguandra and his bride.'

Behind him there was the sound of heavy metal sliding on wood, the double click of a shotgun being cocked.

'Let him be,' Kingdom said, without turning. 'There'll be no trouble, Gus.'

'Not in here,' Haynes agreed. 'This is the day the Hondo Kid gets his come-uppance. I'm calling you out, Kid.'

Kingdom reached back to place his glass on the bar, dropped his cigarette into the sawdust and ground it under his heel.

'You know I've shook hands with your pa, agreed to help him against Aguandra?'

'You're lyin',' Haynes said flatly. 'And you ain't needed. I already downed one of that pack of thieves. Now I aim to get rid of Aguandra's hired gun.'

'You tried with the butt of a six-gun. Now you plan on using the business end, that right?'

'You're hidin' behind words, Hondo,' Haynes said. 'For the second time, I'm callin' you out.'

With a savage grin, Zeke Haynes swung on his heel and left the doors slapping behind him as he pushed through to cross the plankwalk and step down into the dust of West Fork's sun-soaked main street.

12

It was now well past noon. As Boone Kingdom left the Breaker and stepped down off the plankwalk he saw that Zeke Haynes had walked a little way up towards the jailhouse, then turned around to face the eastern end of town with the afternoon sun at his back.

Kingdom took this philosophically, knowing that when a man is facing a fight to the death he will choose the situation most to his advantage. Hell, hadn't he worked that trick himself, more times than he cared to count, in more towns than he could remember?

He walked almost lazily, picking his way over the wagon ruts to the centre of the street. When he turned to face Haynes he noted with some amusement that word had spread — as it always does — and wide-eyed men were tumbling from stores and offices and bursting from the side alleys, their boots clattering along the plankwalks, their voices high-pitched with excitement.

' . . . *Hondo Kid . . . Zeke Haynes called him out . . .* '

' *. . . fool don't stand a chance . . . fastest I ever saw . . .* '

Zeke Haynes moved first. His shadow shifted as he swayed forwards. Then he took a step, and from fifty yards away he began the slow walk that would narrow the distance between them.

He'll want to be real close, Kingdom thought. Point-blank range. He knows he's fast, thinks he can beat me. But he also knows if he don't make his first shot count, he's finished.

Boone Kingdom, the Hondo Kid, began his own slow walk, feeling the hot sun on his face, the taste of dust and salt sweat on his lips, the hard, steady beating of his heart. He was aware of the sinewy play of long leg muscles, the strength yet total relaxation of his arms and hands as they hung loose at his sides, the cool brush of oiled leather against his fingertips. And as he walked, his mind became stilled, the shrill cries of the excited onlookers fading into the background until he was enclosed by a ragged wall of distant sounds that had no meaning.

'That's far enough, Haynes,' he called.

Thirty yards.

Zeke Haynes's stained black vest was open, the lower hem swept back well clear of the upward path of the holstered Colts. In the wide gap between the open vest his cotton shirt was partway unbuttoned, and Kingdom saw the sheen of sweat on pale skin.

'I don't want any part of this, never have, never will,' he said, his low voice shockingly loud in the sudden, awful silence. 'I'm siding with your pa in his fight. Killing you makes no sense. But so you'll know exactly what you're up against, Haynes, here's what I'll do if I'm pushed.'

His right hand moved. Haynes stiffened. The concerted gasp from the onlookers was like the wind sighing through dry salt brush.

Kingdom smiled a sad smile. He said, 'I'll wait until you make your play, Haynes. Better than that, I'll wait until your hands close on your Colts, your fingers curl around the butts — and then I'll wait some more.'

Movement rippled along the watchers as hard men brought up to live and die by the six-gun looked at one another and, muttering, shook their heads in disbelief.

' . . . *ten bucks says he makes it* . . . '

' . . . *greased lightnin' ain't that fast* . . . '

' . . . *my ten says Hondo dies where he stands* . . . '

Remorselessly, Boone Kingdom went on, 'I'll wait until your Colts are out, and lifting, Haynes — and then I'll kill you.'

'You're crazy,' Zeke Haynes said hoarsely. His dark eyes blazed.

'I'll plant a single slug, right there,' Boone Kingdom intoned. His hand came all the way up, pointed. A forefinger jabbed at the glistening flesh revealed by Haynes's open shirt. 'You'll be a dead man before you can squeeze a trigger.'

'You think I'm Ed Jaffe? You think that's what you're up against? Or have you got another friend ready to cut me in two with his shotgun?' Haynes jerked a thumb to where Gus was standing in the doorway of the Breaker. On the plankwalk, somebody sniggered.

'You just don't understand what you're up against, do you, Haynes?' Kingdom said. 'Well, I'm too goddamn tired of all this to explain — so get on with it.'

Beyond Zeke Haynes, Kingdom caught a flicker of movement in the distance and saw the dark suit and white shirt of Dave van Tinteren as the lawyer stepped out of his office.

Then, as if trapped in a dream that had started ten long years ago and tightened its grip to become a never-ending nightmare, Boone Kingdom brought the focus of his gaze back to another gunman who was ready to use his skill with the six-gun in a deadly shoot-out with the Hondo Kid.

A life risked for a reputation: a fleeting glimpse of fame in the shadow of the Reaper.

'You heard me,' Kingdom snarled. 'Get to it, Haynes.'

For a long, wire-taut moment, Zeke Haynes hesitated. His face was beaded with sweat. The bunched muscles in his jaw worked. Kingdom saw the look in his eyes change from seething anger to one of bewilderment and then to something bordering on panic. The tip of Haynes's tongue came out, licked dry lips. What sounded like a dry croak issued from his throat.

Then he made his move.

Both hands were already loosely dangling, brushing the tied-down holsters. Now they flicked upwards, grasped the jutting butts of the Colts. The pistols whispered cleanly out of leather. Haynes's thumbs hooked to cock both hammers as his forefingers squeezed the triggers.

Kingdom saw this. Immobile, as if carved from stone, in that blinding fraction of a second he knew that all Haynes had to do was bring the Colts level and release the hammers. He saw both barrels clear leather. Curiously detached, locked in the slow motion of that recurring nightmare, he watched the revolvers tilt, the yawning holes of the muzzles begin to change shape as the barrels came level and each dark, narrow ellipse widened towards the circular.

Boone Kingdom shot Zeke Haynes in the V of flesh exposed by his open shirt.

A low, sighing moan issued from the lips of the watching men.

Nobody saw Kingdom move. Afterwards, not a man among the onlookers could swear, truthfully, that he had at any time seen a gun in Boone Kingdom's hand.

In a dazzling exhibition of unbelievable speed, Zeke Haynes had flicked both Colts out of their holsters. The smooth movement was not seen, simply registering as a blur alongside those lean hips. But at some point in that tiny, immeasurable fraction of a second before the twin Colts came level, the Hondo Kid drew, fired — and flipped the Remington back into its holster.

The bullet punched home. The sickening sound of its impact was lost in the crack of Kingdom's Remington.

Zeke Haynes's eyes glazed. He rocked back on his heels. His dead thumbs released the hammers, and both slugs ploughed harmlessly into the dust at Boone Kingdom's feet.

' . . . *how the hell! . . .* '

' . . . *Goddamn, I must've blinked! . . .* '

' . . . *did anyone see that? . . .* '

Blood spurted from Zeke Haynes's throat as he fell backwards. He flopped in the dust, slack arms flung wide. One leg twitched. His last living breath was exhaled from between loose lips. Then he was forever still.

With his face set into a bleak mask, seemingly unaware of the sudden wave of sound that began as a hushed whisper then swelled into a roar as the onlookers piled down off the plankwalks to rush across the street and gaze in morbid curiosity at the dead man, Boone Kingdom walked forwards, stepped over Zeke Hayne's limp form and headed up the street.

★ ★ ★

They had shared coffee laced with whiskey, had talked in soft tones, then more acrimoniously as the sun began to sink below the hills of New Mexico and the oil lamps of West Fork washed the bloodstained dust of main street with soft yellow light.

'I watched, and wondered,' Dave van Tinteren said tersely now. 'So many times you've killed similar stupid men, Boone. In all those years, have you found no way to back off?'

'Coming here was to be a release, a way out,' Kingdom said, his face pale in the lamplight, his grey eyes darkly shadowed. 'But important men in West Fork have been actin' devious. If Crabtree had arrested the right man, the law would have taken Haynes's life, not me. If you decide to come clean over what Ike Moss told you, I'll know why Roberto Aguandra wants me dead.'

'But nothing will change.' The lawyer reached up to loosen his black tie, run a finger around the inside of his collar. 'The truth has taken a long time to surface. Ike's an infrequent visitor to West Fork. It was only last year he saw a face, realized something he'd believed over and done with was unfinished in one, tragic detail.'

'Jesus!' Kingdom said, his voice tight with anger and frustration. 'Tragic, you say — yet you keep it to yourself?'

'A tough dilemma, Boone, and I've wrestled with it through more than one sleepless night. What's come out of that

185

hard thinking is that if I keep quiet, nobody gets hurt; if you know the truth there'll be another heavy cross for you to bear. Either way, it won't stop Aguandra, so — '

He broke off as the sudden drum of hooves sounded outside, and as Kingdom swung around to peer out of the uncurtained window he saw Marshal Jim Crabtree draw rein outside the jail-house, tumble from the saddle and hitch his lathered horse to the rail.

The marshal took one hasty look up and down the street, saw the lamplight flooding from van Tinteren's office and came across the street at a run.

Kingdom and the lawyer were on their feet when he burst through the door, slamming it violently back against the wall.

'Easy, Jim,' van Tinteren said.

'It's started,' Crabtree blurted, one hand braced against the wall, his eyes wide.

Kingdom started forward. 'When?'

The marshal shook his head, his chest heaving as he sucked in great gulps of air.

'Too long ago. Aguandra was ready to ride out when I left the Rockin' Z.'

Kingdom stared in disbelief. 'So why come here? Why the hell didn't you ride for the Coldwater, warn High Plains?'

'No.' Crabtree shook his head. 'Isaac already knows what to expect. What he needs now is men with guns.' He squinted at Kingdom, shifted his gaze to van Tinteren and said, 'If we ride now, we could stop a massacre. I could raise a posse, deputize the both of you — but there ain't no time. So, are you with me?'

'I'll get my horse,' Kingdom said. 'Follow me to Dusty's, Marshal, we'll cut across country.' As he started for the door he turned his head, looked at van Tinteren. 'Dave?'

'I'm a lawyer, used to pen and ink and talking myself hoarse — but if you listened to your pa you'll know I can

187

also shoot pretty straight. Let's go.'

The last thing Kingdom saw before he left the office was the lawyer grabbing his hat off the filing cabinet, his gunbelt off the back of the chair.

Then he was out in the street, and running.

13

They heard the crackle of gunfire when cresting a high rise still more than a mile from High Plains, the distant winking of muzzle flashes appearing like clusters of bright stars flickering and dancing too close to the ground.

But there were no stars and, although Boone Kingdom had prophesied that Aguandra would ride in with the moon at his back, there was no moon. The night skies were heavy with swollen rain-clouds, the only light the flare of distant lightning, the only sounds detectable above the beat of the racing hooves the rolling rumble of thunder.

Crabtree had been apprised of the circumstances surrounding the shooting of Zeke Haynes, and had expressed no regrets, but pointed out that it left Isaac short one gun in his battle against Aguandra.

If Aguandra had mustered a full crew to ride against High Plains, he had said grimly, that meant the two remaining horse-ranchers were outnumbered four to one.

'Split up?' Kingdom now called into the wind, and Crabtree urged his racing horse closer, running the risk of a calamitous tumble beneath slashing hooves as he clattered up against Kingdom's stirrup to yell his reply.

'Me and Dave'll circle wide, come at 'em from the flanks,' he cried. 'You go straight in, use them Remingtons to let 'em know you're there, then swing away and go to ground in the scrub.'

'Yeah. Aguandra'll figure one man, maybe the town marshal, send a couple of his hands back from the house.'

'Even the odds,' Crabtree yelled. 'He does that, we'll cut his forces in two!' He leaned recklessly out of the saddle to punch Kingdom's shoulder with a big fist, then veered sharply away into the surrounding darkness.

The deep bellow of the marshal's

voice drifted to Kingdom, rising and falling in volume as the three riders were briefly separated by the dips and ridges of the undulating range. Then another horseman bore down on him, and he caught the flapping of a black coat, the flash of a lifted hand as Dave van Tinteren cut across his back trail and hammered out wide on his right flank.

They were close now. Dark buildings could be distinguished as lightning flickered within the backdrop of black clouds. Excited cries were borne to Kingdom on the wind. The rattle of six-guns was interspersed with the heavier bark of Jake Haynes's buffalo gun and, as he squinted ahead into the gloom, he saw the first crawling flames beginning to lick at the base of the barn's high wooden walls.

But even as he bore down on High Plains, Kingdom knew Jim Crabtree was rattled, his thinking hasty and wrong. Close to the ranch house there was no scrub, no cover of any kind.

That made defence easier for the two men trapped in the house, but left no possibility of a rapid approach and fast withdrawal as envisaged by the marshal.

Also, if Crabtree was planning to race in from the flanks at a gallop, taking Aguandra and his men by storm, he was doomed to failure. Fences completely enclosed High Plains. He and van Tinteren would need to abandon their horses, and risk attacking on foot.

Then Kingdom was jolted back to reality as the sound of the big sorrel's hooves changed from a muted beat to a hard clatter, and the grass underfoot gave way to the packed earth of the trail as he swooped down like a hawk from the last steep rise and crouched low in the saddle to approach the gate.

Even as he did so, the flames licking at the walls of the barn exploded into a vast sheet of fire that roared up and into the air above the roof and sent sparks soaring towards the leaden clouds. High Plains was illuminated as if by a blazing, midday sun. A figure that was surely one of Aguandra's men was caught in the open, sent scuttling like a brown beetle. In the big corral, Jake's wild mustang's coat had the wet sheen of black silk as it reared, hooves flailing. Beyond, in the smaller of the two corrals, the Haynes's saddle horses squealed in fright.

Over to the right, beyond the fences, the land sloped down to Coldwater Creek and the distant stands of trees now starkly picked out by the light from the blazing barn. Across that open land Dave van Tinteren was a mounted shape tearing in towards the far side of the corrals.

But now there was no time for observing.

The stink of hot coal oil and burning wood was in Kingdom's nostrils. Looming high above him, the crosspiece above the gate was a dark line across the raging inferno. Without thought he took the sorrel in through the gate at full gallop. As if by instinct he clamped his knees on the horse, dropped the reins, and both Remingtons leapt into his hands.

Suddenly, the fierce heat from the barn was like a hot wall, terrifying the big sorrel, sending its head back and up. As it ploughed to a stop a six-gun cracked. The bullet hummed past Kingdom's ear, clipped his hair. He triggered both pistols as the scuttling figure appeared almost under the sorrel's nose, and there was a sudden roar of agony.

Away to his left Kingdom saw a body lying face down in the dust, a wagon tipped on its side, its uppermost wheels lazily spinning. There were men crouched behind it, the metal of weapons reflecting the flames, their faces glistening under dark Stetsons, and in that fleeting glance Kingdom recognized Roberto Aguandra.

Then he had used the bright Mexican rowels to snap the sorrel out of its fear and they were past the end of the wagon and closing on the house, the barn a mass of blazing timber seeming to tower perilously above them. He piled out of the saddle, slapped the sorrel hard on its rump, saw it wheel and gallop away from the flames. From the shattered windows under the shadow of the gallery overhang, a six-gun and rifle hammered, and slugs whined over his lowered head as he hit the steps at a run.

'Hold your fire!' Kingdom roared, 'I'm comin' in!'

Hot lead plucked at his shirt as he pounded across the gallery. Behind him a voice with a Mexican accent he recognized as Aguandra's roared, thick with rage, and a volley of bullets slammed into the timber walls. Then the door was snatched open, and Kingdom hurled himself forward, hit the floor on one shoulder to slide across the room on thick animal skins then roll and come to his feet.

The door crashed shut. A heavy wooden bar was slammed into place.

'Welcome to hell,' Isaac Haynes said

drily. He was down on one knee by the table, his head bent as he fumbled to reload his Colt. One sleeve of his buckskin jacket was blood-soaked, but when he glanced up his dark eyes blazed with the light of battle and Kingdom knew that with the agonizing spell of waiting over and done with, he was a man with a purpose.

The only way Roberto Aguandra would get High Plains was over Isaac Haynes's dead body.

'Crabtree and van Tinteren are out there somewhere,' Kingdom said, and over at the window Jake Haynes laughed.

'We downed two of the bastards before you got here. You plugged another, rode straight over him. I reckon the odds are about even.'

'We'd outnumber 'em if Zeke was here,' Isaac said. Again he glanced up at Kingdom and, as he snapped the Colt's cylinder home, there was a question in the blazing dark eyes, maybe even a premonition, and Boone

Kingdom clamped his jaw shut and turned away because now, surely, was not the time.

Again a volley of shots slammed into the solid walls. Most of the remaining broken glass tinkled from the windows. Jake Haynes popped his head and shoulders up, blasted a single shot from his long rifle, then let it clatter to the boards.

'Too slow,' he said, reaching for his six-gun, and Kingdom strode to the front of the house, flattened himself against the wall alongside the other window and peered out at the yard drenched with yellow, flickering light from the leaping flames.

'They broke down the doors, wheeled that wagon out of the barn,' Isaac Haynes said at his shoulder. 'Tipped it, been usin' it for cover ever since.' He chuckled. 'Chose well, damn them. I built it with my own hands, and with Jake's buff' gun dumped there ain't no slugs gonna penetrate those boards.'

'But now they're pinned down,'

Kingdom said. He snapped three quick shots from the Remington in his right hand, saw an arm poke around the end of the wagon and ducked back as a six-gun blazed. He grinned at Haynes as the slugs hummed through the window and thunked into the back wall. 'That's the best they can do. Only way they can get out from behind that wagon is by creatin' some kind of diversion.'

'They fired the barn,' Isaac said. 'Figured that might do it.'

'No.' Kingdom shook his head. 'That was for light.'

'Then they did real well,' Jake said with heavy sarcasm. 'All them flames have done is show us where they're at.'

'Bright enough for me to see Aguandra,' Kingdom agreed, frowning. 'But where's Harry Gregg?'

'For that matter,' Isaac Haynes said, 'where the hell's Crabtree and van Tinteren?'

'Takin' Aguandra from the flanks — but I always did feel that was wrong. If they've got sense they'll back-track, come in the direct route through the gate.'

And Kingdom had a hunch that was exactly what they would do. Dave van Tinteren would have been balked by the fences, forced to go round. Crabtree would have hit the same problem, and neither man would have relished abandoning their horses that far out.

Suddenly, from the end of the wagon furthest from the flames, a man emerged. Ducked low, he triggered one hasty shot towards the windows then sprinted desperately for the deep shadows at the side of the house.

Almost casually, Boone Kingdom threw down with the Remington in his left hand. The shot cracked. In a boiling eruption of dust caught in the glare the man tumbled heavily, rolled, and lay still.

'Jesus Christ!' Isaac Haynes breathed, his awed tones almost drowned by the roar of the flames.

'And now they're outnumbered,' Jake Haynes gloated, his voice edged with triumph.

From behind the wagon, Roberto Aguandra suddenly roared, 'Now, Gregg!'

Flummoxed, Jake popped up to take a look, and from the other end of the wagon a gun flamed. Jake grunted deep down, reeled backwards, cannoned into one of the big chairs. He slumped against it, upper body on the cushioned seat, his spread legs on the floor. Blood began to soak the front of his shirt. His eyes were wide, unseeing, his mouth slack.

Wild-eyed, Isaac Haynes covered the intervening space in a couple of long strides, sank down by his son. As he did so the kitchen door was kicked open with a splintering crash and big Harry Gregg leaped into the room, catching the big rancher on his knees, Kingdom with both Remingtons pointing at the floor.

'Hold it right there,' he roared. His

craggy, moustachioed face was set cold and hard. A cocked, levelled six-gun jutted from each big fist. 'You, Hondo, pouch those guns.'

'That means bringin' them up. I do that, you're dead, Gregg.'

'Naw. I've got the triggers squeezed back, hammers held by a whisker. Even you ain't that fast, Hondo.'

For the blink of an eye, Kingdom hesitated. Then he took a breath, flipped the Remingtons over and spun them into their holsters.

'Unfasten the belt?'

Gregg grinned, shook his head. 'I'm too old to hanker after a reputation, but let's say I'm curious. You want to make your play, you're welcome to try.'

On the other side of the room, Isaac Haynes coughed as the acrid smoke of gunpowder and burning timber caught at his throat. 'Jake'll live,' he rasped, 'but this madness has already killed good men. How many's left alive out there, Gregg?'

'Two. But it's finished, over. You'll

be off High Plains within the hour, Haynes.' Then, lifting his chin, he yelled, 'Come on in, Aguandra!'

'You're too late,' Boone Kingdom said suddenly. He was listening, his head half turned towards the windows, and he felt a surge of triumph as the beat of hooves swelled rapidly and he knew his hunch had been right. 'Aguandra moves, now,' he said, 'he won't make the front door. Those horses you hear approaching belong to Crabtree and van Tinteren. They're comin' through the gate. It's over, sure, Gregg — all over for the Rockin' Z.'

As the beat of hooves hammered across the yard, the four men became frozen, as if locked in thought, or stunned disbelief. The light from the flames engulfing the big barn flickered eerily across the walls, creating shifting shadows that leaped from floor to ceiling like tormented demons. The smoke from the fierce blaze had drifted in through the shattered windows and curled, wraithlike, around the smoking oil lamps that had miraculously survived the gunfire.

A fusillade rattled out. A man yelled, the cry trailing away into a thin wail that ended in silence. Another voice shouted, unintelligible but choked with fury. And then, 'Watch him, Dave, goddamn it, he's gettin' away!'

'Marshal Crabtree,' Boone Kingdom said softly. 'Aguandra's gettin' clear, so now I guess it's your move, Gregg.'

'Hell, I never did fancy no strap-steel cage,' Harry Gregg said. 'But then I never shot a man down in cold blood — and it looks like that's the only way I'll get out of here.'

'No,' Kingdom said. 'I don't accommodate fools, Gregg, but I hate leavin' a man with his curiosity unsatisfied. So, if you've got them Colts lined up and ready — '

Still talking casually, Boone Kingdom stepped sideways and began his draw.

All Harry Gregg needed to do was shift his thumbs off the Colt's cocked hammers. What faced Kingdom was the need to pluck two heavy Remingtons from leather holsters, then lift them and trigger two shots before those hammers fell.

To Isaac Haynes, crouched low, eyes bleary from the effects of smoke and the message reaching his brain confused by the flickering light and dancing shadows, it seemed that the Remingtons simply appeared in Boone Kingdom's hands.

The balls of Harry Gregg's thumbs slid off warm metal. The Hondo Kid's hands must have dipped down, and come up. And as four shots rang out as one, reverberating thunderously off the four walls, in the centre of Gregg's forehead two black holes appeared and he went backwards into the splintered door, and slid lifeless to the floor.

Into the hushed, leaden silence, Isaac Haynes said, 'If I live to be a hundred, I swear . . . ' And his voice trailed away as he became lost for words.

Boone Kingdom was picking himself up when the front door banged open and Jim Crabtree burst into the room.

'Dave's gone to settle the horses,' he said, his blue eyes sweeping the room. 'Looks like everyone's alive in here — just.' He shook his head. 'Aguandra — '

'I'll go,' Kingdom cut in.

'Headed towards the Coldwater,' Crabtree said. 'Likely cross, then swing west and ride fast for the border, abandon the Rockin' Z for good.'

'Later, maybe. But not now. He wants me more than he wanted High Plains,' Kingdom said. 'Old Ike Moss knows why, but he's headed south. So does Dave van Tinteren, but he ain't tellin'. Now I aim to find out from Aguandra.'

He pushed past the marshal and went down the steps into the heat and light of the yard. At his shrill whistle the sorrel came trotting towards him through the swirling smoke. Boone Kingdom tossed the loose reins over the big horse's head, stepped up into the saddle, and rode past the tipped wagon and the limp bodies lying sprawled in the dust and headed out of High Plains and down the long slope towards the trees.

14

The roar of the flames consuming the barn faded behind Boone Kingdom as he took the sorrel down the long slope at an easy canter. His shadow lengthened, rippling darkly over the uneven grassland. Thunder rumbled in the distance, but the threat of rain had passed as the clouds moved away towards the mountains. The moon drifted into clear skies, briefly washing the grass with light before again floating behind a lingering cloud.

At the western edge of the trees, Coldwater Creek was a faint metallic sheen visible beyond the darker mass of land. But Kingdom knew that the surface of those waters would be undisturbed. Roberto Aguandra had not crossed, and if Jim Crabtree had seen him ride in this direction there was only one sensible place for him to wait for the man he had sworn to kill.

The faint breeze whispered through the willows and taller cottonwood trees as Kingdom approached. In the light from the fire, still blazing strongly like a triumphant beacon marking Isaac Haynes's High Plains, the wind-tossed leaves appeared like a shimmering, multi-toned silvery-grey wall.

A broken wall.

Where the tall grass and weeds had been cut and trampled by hooves and the low branches snapped to leave pale, jagged stumps, Boone Kingdom ducked low in the saddle and entered the woods. At once, he was enfolded in darkness, felt his pulse quicken and his nostrils flare instinctively at the smell of damp wood and mouldering leaves, the faint aroma of cigar smoke.

Again giving the sorrel its head, he squinted into the gloom as leafy branches brushed his shoulders, his face, and the horse blew softly as it picked a route through the trees.

Somewhere ahead, another horse nickered.

Kingdom reached down to brush the oiled holsters, let his palms feel the cool of the Remington's butts; grasped them, eased them in the slick leather, then dropped his hands to wipe them dry on the rough cloth of his pants.

Then the trees began to thin. A cool breeze touched his face. Almost without warning, the sorrel emerged into a clearing illuminated by the distant flickering of the fire and high skies made luminous by the fickle moon.

'Ten years,' Roberto Aguandra called clearly.

'That has meaning for me,' Kingdom said. 'What about you?'

He slid down from the saddle, slapped the sorrel to send it trotting away, walked slowly forwards, his boots rustling through dry leaves.

Roberto Aguandra was standing at the far side of the clearing — no more than forty feet away — alongside unnatural, low mounds almost hidden

209

by the undergrowth that had proliferated under the trees. He was a dark figure almost lost against the thick blackness of the woods. A cigar glowed in his left hand, the gold of heavy rings glinted on his fingers.

Ten feet from the rancher, watching the hard glitter in the man's eyes, the poised readiness of his lax right hand, Kingdom stopped.

'No bodies,' he said absently, remembering van Tinteren's words about what Dusty Rhodes had found — or not found — at John Kingdom's spread, thinking also of Jake Haynes talking about life at High Plains. '*We cut timber in them woods*,' he had said, '*for building and such like*,' and, suddenly understanding, Kingdom nodded towards the mounds and said, 'Before that day was out, you came here to bury the men who killed my folks. You were content with that, while their graves remained hidden. But the Hayneses had been cutting timber for years, and were getting too close. That's why you moved now, after a long silence. That's why you wanted High Plains.'

'They were my brothers,' Roberto Aguandra said, his voice thick with emotion, a quiver there, too, as if he was keeping a tight rein on anger. 'I laid them to rest. That rest was about to be disturbed . . . '

Boone Kingdom took a deep breath. 'All right. It took a day's toil for me to bury my folks, so I can understand your feelings — but not the bullheaded way you tried to put things right.' He watched the path of the glowing cigar as Aguandra lifted it to his lips, the brighter glow as he inhaled, the sudden swift arc of light as the rancher flicked it away; felt his muscles tense as the rancher stepped away from the trees.

'No, Kingdom,' Aguandra said tightly, furiously, 'you don't understand one goddamn thing!'

'I was fifteen years old when your brothers murdered my folks,' Kingdom said. 'Out of necessity, fired by grief

211

and anger, I moved faster than your kid brother packin' the shotgun, faster than your two brothers toting six-guns — one of 'em wearin' the hat he stole from my pa. I guess I pulled two guns faster than any man, anywhere, any time — but I've got no fight with you, Aguandra.'

'You're wrong.'

Kingdom shook his head. 'I'm right. You want revenge for what I did, but that's your fight, not mine. I don't blame any man for crimes committed by his kin.'

'Supposing,' Roberto Aguandra hissed, 'supposing I told you it was me stole your pa's hat — what then?'

'You?' Kingdom felt the hairs on his scalp prickle. He saw the flash of Aguandra's teeth as the man grinned ferociously, the pale movement of his naked right hand that was already hovering too close to the fancy holster at his hip. But his thoughts were whirling, his wits too dulled to sense the menace.

'No,' he said, stupidly, uncomprehendingly, his mind struggling to backtrack through ten years of frozen memories to the time when a boy had listened — listened, not looked — as three renegades gunned down his folks, then watched, but from a distance and with his mind numbed with grief and anger, as they rode away.

'If you stole my pa's hat,' he said hoarsely, 'then you killed my pa — and that ain't possible because I killed those three men.'

'Four of us,' Aguandra spat. 'Four men. One too young, so we left him behind. Three of us went on to gun down a stupid nester who wouldn't give us what gold he'd got stashed away, was so protective of his pretty wife he was ready for them both to die rather than let us get close.'

'I got there,' Boone Kingdom said numbly, 'but too late.'

'We rode away with the cabin blazing,' Aguandra went on relentlessly, 'came back later, all four of us, figurin' when the fire had cooled we could search for the cache we knew was there — '

'There was no cache, no gold — '

'The kid wanted your pa's hat. I gave it to him . . . ' Aguandra's voice trailed away. Under the white shirt that was stained with dust and sweat his broad chest heaved as he dragged in gulps of cool night air. The glittering black eyes were blinking fast, seeing only memories.

'I gave it to him,' he repeated dully. 'I gave the kid your pa's hat, planted it on his head — and then my horse went lame and I was left behind to live.' He laughed suddenly, wildly. 'You killed the wrong man, Kingdom — and it was all my goddamn fault!'

Roberto Aguandra leaped sideways and went for his gun while Boone Kingdom was still grappling with the awful truth; brought it up and level while Kingdom's eyes were still naked with horror.

The first shot lit the clearing with

bright flame. The bullet punched into Boone Kingdom high above the left elbow and slammed him backwards, spinning him, shafting a bolt of agony through his shoulder.

The backwards spin saved his life.

Fanning the Colt's hammer, Roberto Aguandra loosed three fast shots. One plucked at Kingdom's shirt. A second whisked his hat high. The third whistled through the tall trees.

Then Kingdom moved. He moved in the way he had grown accustomed to moving in the shabby border towns he had passed through in the ten long years since he had gunned down the Aguandra brothers: both hands dipped for the oiled holsters holding the Remingtons, at a speed that had always been too fast for the eye to follow.

But this time one hand lagged. In that fraction of a second he was vaguely aware that his left hand refused to answer the signal, instead sending a wave of pain through his body and causing a rushing in his ears that weakened his knees, sent him swaying dizzily.

None of that mattered.

Even as he swayed, loose-limbed, the right Remington was up, spitting flame, and Roberto Aguandra was driven backwards, staggering through the leaves, staggering back towards the three mounds, until his boot heels struck the hard, risen earth and he fell, dead, across the graves of his long-dead brothers.

* * *

It was 1868. Two men had witnessed the fulfilment of a six-gun legend but, fittingly, only one had lived. And as he whistled weakly to his horse, struggled awkwardly into the saddle and swung the big sorrel towards the gap in the woods and rode back up the slope towards the high, blazing barn, Boone Kingdom vowed that the Remington .44s he had used to live that legend would, by daybreak, once again repose in the red-lined box in Dave van Tinteren's West Fork office.

THE END

We do hope that you have enjoyed reading this large print book.

Did you know that all of our titles are available for purchase?

We publish a wide range of high quality large print books including:
**Romances, Mysteries, Classics, General Fiction,
Non Fiction and Westerns.**

Special interest titles available in large print are:
**The Little Oxford Dictionary
Music Book, Song Book
Hymn Book, Service Book**

Also available from us courtesy of Oxford University Press:
**Young Readers' Dictionary
(large print edition)
Young Readers' Thesaurus
(large print edition)**

For further information or a free brochure, please contact us at:
**Ulverscroft Large Print Books Ltd.,
The Green, Bradgate Road, Anstey,
Leicester, LE7 7FU, England.
Tel:** (00 44) **0116 236 4325
Fax:** (00 44) **0116 234 0205**